RAGE

AGAINST

the

DYING LIGHT

RAGE

AGAINST

the

DYING LIGHT

A Novel

JAN SURASKY

Jacket design and Illustration by
Rob Wood, Wood Ronsaville Harlin, Inc.

Interior book design by Susan Surasky

Library of Congress Cataloging-in-Publication Card Number:
TXu1-261-405

No part of this book may be used or reproduced in any manner whatsoever
without written permission.

Published by Sandalwood Press
Victor, New York

© Jan Surasky. All rights reserved.
Printed in the United States of America
ISBN 978-0-578-00367-2

To children everywhere —

May they always dream.

Do not go gentle into that good night,
. . . Rage, rage against the dying of the light.

-*Dylan Thomas*

RAGE

AGAINST

the

DYING LIGHT

Acknowledgments

I would like to thank those who have been closest to me as readers for my magazine articles, those who have had a hand in critiquing this manuscript, and those who have provided encouragement to persist in sharing this tale through the written word.

I would like to thank Book1One for their help in the technical aspects of readying this manuscript for publication.

I would like to thank Marcia Blitz for her creative flap and back cover copy and for her upbeat spirit.

I would also like to thank the firm of Wood, Ronsaville, and Harlan. Rob Wood for his very beautiful and imaginative cover design, Pam Ronsaville for her consummate art direction and ready understanding, Kassie Wood for her cheerful, persistent patience, and all of them for their many kindnesses and courtesies.

Forenote

As I began this book and collected histories on Celtic life, I found that many of them disagreed with each other. Although most held the same photographs of Celtic artifacts found in archeological digs on the British isles, interpretations differed.

The Celts left us no written word. We have an eyewitness account of British Celtic customs written by Caesar during his failed attempt to occupy their island, about fifty years before Boudicca's birth. We have the *Annals of Tacitus* written about fifty years after Boudicca's death, and a history of Rome written by Cassius Dio one hundred years later. Both contain descriptions of Boudicca and her rebellion. These three are written from the point of view of the Roman conqueror.

I could only imagine how Boudicca might have lived. The facts of battle, not only Boudicca's struggle to rid her beloved isle of the conquering Romans, but the battles of her contemporaries Caractacus, Venutius and Cartimandua, are faithful to the Roman accounts cited above. Following is her story.

J.S.

Chapter One

Catrinellia bustled about the long, low table, bossing servants in the Coritani palace's great hall. Her regal bearing, so steadily in evidence as a Celtic queen, had momentarily been intercepted by a strong desire to personally oversee preparations for tonight's banquet. To this end, she fussed at the servants, instructing one to exchange a silver serving platter with carefully sculpted inlaid fish swimming after each other around the rim for a larger, more elaborate, gold one with warriors and chariots, spears at the ready, engaging in battle; another, to bring out a larger serving bowl, one with chunks of amber embedded in the sides and exquisitely chiseled animal heads with coral-studded eyes peering out from under the rim; and, yet another, to set out more wine flagons.

The Silures would arrive this afternoon and Catrinellia knew the importance of a favorable meeting. As queen to the Coritani chieftain Votorix, she knew an alliance with the Silures would help to strengthen the security of the Coritani against the threat of their more warlike southern neighbors the Cautevellani. But, everyone knew how difficult it was to get two Celtic chieftains to agree, especially on politics. Catrinellia hoped that a great, welcoming feast, in the true Celtic tradition, would soften the Silures.

The Silures contingent was an important one. Cunobelinus himself was coming, chief of a tribe that, under his great-grandfather, had stood against the Roman army nearly a hundred years before. Caractacus, his oldest son and royal heir, would be there as well, along with Venutius, a royal ward from the Iberian Deceangli tribe, and the most elite nobles and most honored generals.

She lifted the skirts of her long olive-grey tunic slightly to whisk her tall, agile body more efficiently over the expanse of the high-ceilinged great hall's clay floors. She must check the pantry and the larder, and make certain that the hearth was readied and the spits prepared.

In the hallway outside the great hall, her daughter, the princess Boudicca, stood peering in at the flurry of preparations. To Boudicca, newly-turned sixteen, it was too soon to practice the formalities of queenly duties, at least on a regular basis. Her brother Mandorix, ten years her junior, who so often pestered her for a game of hide the boar's tooth, was at play in the palace courtyard. She turned and slipped unnoticed down the hallway and out the palace's great front iron gates.

The city of the Celtic Coritani tribe stood on a hill overlooking the fertile plains of the northern British countryside. Laid out in the typical Celtic manner, its palace was at one end, its merchants' and artisans' shops and homes lined the narrow streets at the other, and the homes of its nobility and military leaders were set off to the side.

The city looked out over a large expanse of fields and farmers' small, round, thatched clay huts. The fields, rich with grain, were interspersed with large and modest herds of cattle, pigs, and flocks of sheep. It also overlooked the Devon River, which ran down to the North Sea, and which brought succulent fish of all types to the Coritani table.

Boudicca passed through the large, open gate of the stone and timber walls which surrounded the city, with a slow, measured stride. But, as soon as she reached the steep hillside which gave rise to the city, and gazed down upon the meadow which stretched below it, she broke into the run which had given her so much childish pleasure. As she raced down the hillside toward the sacred grove at the far end of the meadow, Boudicca thought of Diviticus. He would be certain to be full of news after his journey to the Isle of Mona for the Druids' annual meeting. And, she would be the first to hear it, even before her father. Diviticus had been her friend since childhood, and always had time to share his Druid wisdom with her, even when Mama and Papa were too busy to satisfy her insatiable curiosity.

Her long, red tresses sparkled in the sun, flowing free about her shoulders, as she ran across the meadow through the newly risen spring violets. She would dress her hair for tonight's banquet in the formal Celtic manner, she thought, but for now, she savored the wind running through it. She arrived at the edge of the grove, and made her way through the stand of sacred oak trees to Diviticus' small, clay hut.

As she reached his hut, Diviticus emerged, ducking as he passed through the small doorway. Outside, the rays of the sun that passed through the trees bounced off his long, blond locks, making the grey that ran through them sparkle. He straightened his long robes as he brought himself up to his full height. The lines that ran through his face, reflecting years of study, lifted somewhat as he saw Boudicca running toward him.

"Diviticus, Diviticus," gasped Boudicca, out of breath as she reached his hut, "what did you bring me?"

"Now, Boudicca," he smiled, slightly, "do you think I went all the way to Mona just to bring you back a gift?"

"Diviticus," she repeated, ignoring his gentle teasing, and throwing her arms around him, "where did you hide it?"

"Well, I guess I will have to surrender it," he said, as he took her hand and drew her inside his hut. There, next to his traveling pack was a small, carved, wooden object. He lifted it gently and handed it to Boudicca.

"Oh, Diviticus," she said, quieting suddenly as she stared down at a small, oaken carving of the Celtic fertility goddess. "What a beautiful likeness of Sequanna."

"It was a pleasant way to pass the lonely nights by the campfire on my journey to Mona," he answered, smiling at her pleasure.

"Now I will have my own image of Sequanna to bedeck with flowers come Beltane," she said. The vision of her own flower-bedecked idol increased her anticipation of the spring rites festival she cherished the most among Celtic customs.

She knew the carving was Diviticus' way to gently remind her that someday she would be a Celtic queen. Then it would be necessary to secure Sequanna's favors for the blessings of royal heirs and a bountiful tribal harvest. But, for now, she wanted only to continue learning at Diviticus' knee and to roam the mossy, anemone-filled floor of the sacred grove. She wanted only to ponder life from her favorite tree stump healed over after a centuries-old stroke of lightning. And, to make friends with the hares that roamed the glade.

"Diviticus," she begged, "tell me about your journey to Mona."

She settled herself cross-legged on the clay floor next to Diviticus, who had already perched himself on a sturdy, three-legged hearth stool, one of the few furnishings to grace his simple hut.

"I traveled through the land of the Brigantes to the Isle of Mona," he began. "Everywhere there were herds of pigs and sheep. The Brigantes are a large and warlike tribe, grown strong from the heritage of their ancestors in the mountains of the Continent. But, for now, on our island, they are content to herd their sheep and plow their fields."

"What are their people like," she asked. She fixed her blue eyes intently upon his face, waiting for his account which would bring her news of the world beyond the Coritani kingdom.

Diviticus chuckled. Despite the maturity of her body, her eagerness to share his travels remained the same when as a child she sat upon his lap and listened to his tales, and nibbled the honey he had gathered along the way, and packed so carefully for her in his knapsack. "The people," he said, "are sturdy, hard-working, and generous. I spent many nights around their fires, and often under their roofs. They shared a hearty rye bread, baked from the grain they grow in abundance, an occasional wild fowl, fish from their streams, and a rich, creamy goat cheese made from a recipe handed down from their Swiss ancestors on the Continent."

"After their meals, they often have trials of valor, as we do," he continued. "The bards and the vates celebrate the hero with wine and song."

Boudicca's eyes sparkled, picturing the Brigantes in the country north of the Coritani.

"They are a strong tribe, with many cities," he added. "Velorix has ruled with great wisdom, for many decades, but he is old now. Cartimandua will soon be queen."

It had been many years since Boudicca had seen Cartimandua. The Brigantes heiress to the throne had often accompanied Velorix on his travels to the Coritani palace for inter-tribal chieftain gatherings. But, now Velorix was ill and did not travel.

Since she was old enough, Boudicca had often romped in the woods with visiting heirs of Celtic kingdoms, many of whom had visited only once and by now had passed out of her memory entirely. But, Cartimandua, the Silures prince Caractacus, and his foster brother Venutius had been frequent visitors.

Caractacus and Venutius, two years older than she, had always shared their companionship with her, often roaming the sacred grove for woodland treasures. A stream which washed the body and the spirit, a hare which foretold the future of the Celtic race. But, Cartimandua, four years her elder, preferred to remain separate, seating herself on an undisturbed fallen log, often accompanied by two or three of her carefully-bred golden hounds. Sometimes, she would seat herself on a three-legged stool hauled to the woodland by a handmaiden, while the servant held a mirror, scrolled in gold and inlaid with coral, to her face, and replaced the strands of ebony hair that had escaped from the elaborate hair-do, or smoothed the wrinkles of her intricately-woven tunic. Often, she passed the time listening to the tunes of a Brigantes court jester, whose musical poems she shared with the others only when they were worn from their woodland jaunts.

Sometimes, Caractacus hunted in the woodlands and shared his hunting skills with his companions. An expert marksman since youth, his blond, good looks depicted the traditional Celtic warrior. He brought down only game which matched the Celtic tradition, sparing the sacred goose and allowing the white hare to run free. Venutius, with the darker looks of the Iberian Celt, more thoughtful but sometimes quicker to anger than his foster brother, shared with her his skill in carving a bow and an arrow from a young, green sapling tree-limb. When the seasons grew full of idle hours without the pleasures of her companions, Boudicca sent arrows wafting onto the wind or toward the circles she drew on the birches and pines with woodland stones.

"Diviticus," asked Boudicca, fixing her gaze again intently upon his twinkling, blue eyes, "what was the talk of at Mona?"

Diviticus' eyes turned serious as he leaned toward her upon his stool and fixed his gaze upon her once again. "We Druids recounted tales of tribal disputes and discussed just methods of settling them. The disputes of warring tribes. Land disputes among the farmer, merchant disputes, military disputes, and even royal household disputes.

"We discussed religious rites and omens. Which omens held the most promise and how best to extract the signs of augury from them. This last brought hot dispute from Xianthus of the Venuti and Triantho of the Cautevellani, which lasted until the sun rose twice, on the merits of right or left passage of a white hare under the stars of a midnight sky."

"But," he added, leaning forward, "the talk was mostly on the fear of Roman attack, and the fear of Roman rule, as our Italian, Gallic, and Iberian cousins have suffered for nearly a century. When Caesar grew tired of attempting to subdue us in tandem

7

with our Gallic neighbors, while they tried his patience with uprisings and drew his fleet, sorely in need of repairs, from our shores, he left with only a loose alliance from two of Briton's Celtic tribes. There is talk that our undefeated isle is a challenge to some of the Roman senate."

"It is said," he continued, "that the Roman emperor Tiberius does not love power and rules justly and wisely. He opposes the gladiator games and does not lust for the acquisition of lands across the sea. But, gladiator matches and expanding the Roman empire are causes dear to the hearts of the Roman senate and to those who wield the power in Rome, and it is feared that there will be attempts upon his life, or attempts to depose him in favor of a more aggressive emperor."

For Boudicca, Caesar's conquest of Gaul in 55 BC, nearly a hundred years before, and his two attempts upon Briton, nearly a year apart, seemed like ancient history. Although she had heard the story of Caesar's landings celebrated in story and song, it melded into the rich and colorful tales of the many exploits of several thousand years in the history of her Celtic ancestors. Of battles and migrations. Of stands against invaders. Of victory. Of the sacking of Rome.

But, what stood in her mind was not the Roman subjugation of Italia, Iberia, and Gaul. It was the earlier attack of Rome upon the Celtic mountain tribes of Germania, where the Celts repelled the Roman armies, remaining free of domination. It was there she was certain that her direct ancestors lay, since the tales of their valor in the face of a highly disciplined Roman army, were full of flaming-haired warriors.

To Diviticus, the fear of Roman attack rose often as he gazed upon the undisturbed meadows of the ancient countryside, the fields tended by serfs who labored under the sun to bring grain from the once fallow soil, and the ancient groves where Druids agonized over justice and practiced the rites of their ancestors which had been handed down through hundreds of centuries.

Diviticus had learned of Caesar's landing on British soil at the knee of his grandfather who, as a young man barely into his twenties, had stood against Caesar's armies. His grandfather spun visions of Celtic warriors who fought with valor and a Roman army driven by discipline and sheer numbers. He told of battles of Celtic tribe against Celtic tribe, which pressed the Cautevellani and Trinovantes to seek Caesar's aid, a favor they paid for with loose alliance to Rome, which they still honored. The fear of Roman armies returning to claim the remaining British Celtic tribes as trophies of the Roman empire, as the western territories of the Continent had proved to be since defeat, seemed always to be ominous.

"It was thought by many Druids that the way to repel the Roman threat was for all of Briton's Celtic tribes to unite to form one nation," continued Diviticus. "But," he mused, "there are those who also believe that we will sooner see the sun set in the east than see all the Celtic tribes of Briton unite under a single banner."

Boudicca listened with patience to Diviticus' talk of politics. She knew it was his way to tell her that one day she would be wed to a Celtic chieftain and, as queen, would be expected to support tribal policy. But, the lush song of the woodland thrush and the faintly perfumed scent of the violets which filled the mossy floor of the ancient grove brought memories of Caractacus' and Venutius' visits past, and visions of their promised stay.

"Diviticus," she said, a smile flashing across her once intense countenance, "Caractacus and Venutius will soon be here."

Diviticus smiled. The joy of her anticipation to roam the sacred grove with her long-time companions filled the room. "Boudicca," he said, gently leaning toward her, "Caractacus and Venutius accompany Cunobelinus on a serious mission. They will sit long in the Coritani council."

"But," she answered, "I must show Caractacus how fat the furry, white hare has got we found as a newborn babe. And," she added, "show Venutius how high the oak has risen we planted from the acorn in the clearing at the edge of the sacred grove."

"And I," he laughed, "must show them the new method we learned at Mona to guide our journey by the stars. But, first," he added, "we must know how important is their visit to the Coritani. Cunobelinus comes to talk of alliance against the threat of warring Celtic tribes. The Silures would build strength with an ally in the north, and the Coritani with the Silures numbers.

"Cunobelinus grows old, and Caractacus will inherit the reign of the Silures tribe. He must sit in council and listen to the talk of affairs of state. He must listen to the nobles and the generals. One day he will be asked to make decisions weighty to the Silures, and perhaps to the destiny of other tribes as well.

"Venutius must also sit in council. As foster son to a royal household, he must abide by the same duties as the king's son. Cunobelinus, in Iberia to seal a trade treaty, saved from the attack of Roman brigands by Venutius' father King Erithrominus, in gratitude promised to educate the young prince as his own first-born son. Blood member of a royal household on soil where Celtic monarchy has been diminished by the Romans, Venutius is trained to one day be prince consort to a Celtic tribe on our own isle. He, too, must grow wise in tribal ways."

Boudicca smiled at Diviticus' gentle reminder of royal duties. "I will amuse myself while the Silures meet in council around the long tables of the great hall," she promised. "But," she added, a smile playfully racing across her face, "When the nobles and generals are easy with ale and the music of the minstrels and bards, I will draw Caractacus and Venutius to our sacred grove. In a fortnight it will be Beltane, and they must help me choose a crown of mistletoe from the sacred oak for my first bonfire dance of maidens to honor the goddess Sequanna."

Diviticus chuckled. "I will save the glossiest and choicest vines for your choosing," he promised. "It is a great honor to enter the rank of the Celtic maiden."

"Diviticus," she asked, "will you sit in council with the Silures?"

"No," he answered, as his brow creased slightly in thought, "I will not be asked to sit in council to seal a treaty between tribes. But, I will be consulted if the Silures and Coritani do not reach agreement. I must be prepared to appease the desires of both sides, to bring a settlement between tribes unequal in numbers but willing to stand together against the attack of a warring tribe."

Boudicca smiled as she rose to leave and threw her arms about Diviticus once again. "I shall treasure always my likeness of Sequanna," she said, as she lifted the carefully carved wooden idol into her hands and passed through the doorway of the modest hut and out into the thickly wooded grove. As she reached the edge, she turned to wave to Diviticus, but he had already passed into the mist of the rays of the afternoon sun.

Out onto the meadow and into the full rays of the sun, Boudicca headed toward the banks of the Devon River. Perhaps she would find Linnea, daughter of the tenant farmer Corianthus, in an idle moment from her chores as the eldest in a large, farmer's family. Linnea had been her friend since they had discovered each other on the banks of the nearby river in search of the first cowslips and baby blackbirds of spring. Since that time they had spent many seasons wandering the plains and meadows together, in search of each season's bounty, the first daisies of spring, the hollow behind a rock of a winter hare. Used to the long hours of labor of the Celtic farmer's family, Linnea bore long, blond tresses crowning a hearty build. But, her tinkling laughter was as delicate as the strains of a minstrel's lyre.

Linnea was her birth twin, born as many seasons ago, and in the same phase of the moon. Together they would join the maiden's dance of Beltane. They had been preparing for many years, in girlish whispers and giggles among the gold of the daffodils along the banks of the Devon River and under the mistletoe that hung heavy with plump, white berries on the oaks of the sacred grove in the chill of winter winds.

Boudicca's eyes sparkled as visions of the spring rites dance crowded her thoughts. Maidens bedecked with flowers and crowned in mistletoe dancing about a bonfire to the strains of the minstrels' lyres, tossing freshly gathered woodland violets and daisies of the first spring rain at the feet of the life-sized likeness of the Celtic fertility goddess, carefully sculpted from the oak of the sacred grove. Tunics the hues of spring blossoms, the bright gold of the marsh daffodils, the pale pink of the wild anemone, and the deep purple of the woodland violet.

Boudicca lifted her tunic to run down the grassy slope of the River Devon's banks. She searched for Linnea as she ran, spotting her sprawled among the bright yellow of the gorse, her simple, homespun linen tunic casually about her, as she watched a frog sunning itself on one of the rocks which lined the edge of the river, home to the salmon, the bass, and the brown, speckled trout. She ran to the spot where her friend lay and dropped down beside her, puffing from the long, downhill run.

"Linnea, Linnea," she gasped, "Caractacus and Venutius arrive before sundown."

Linnea lifted herself to sit cross-legged, giggling at her friend's joy. "What will you wear?" she asked.

"Oh, Linnea," she answered, "I have hardly given a moment's thought to a costume for tonight's banquet. I must hurry back to choose a proper tunic. Mama will expect me to appear fittingly dressed for tonight's festivities," she added, pouting only slightly at the decided inconvenience of more formal attire.

"But, first," laughed Linnea, "I must see who I shall marry." She pulled a yellow daisy firmly from its place along the grassy bank. "Will it be Anthropus or Granorix?" she asked, tossing a daisy petal over her left shoulder and naming two sons to tenant farmers. "Anthropus is strong and a hard worker. And, he is so handsome. But, he is shy. Granorix is not as hard a worker, but he is bolder." She paused. "Oh, I hope it's Anthropus," she giggled, adding wistfully, "I hope his dowry is big enough when Papa chooses. Papa says we need a big dowry with nine mouths to feed."

Linnea finished pulling the daisy petals one by one, tossing them over her left shoulder as she and Boudicca giggled at the suspense of the simple, girlish exercise. "Oh, look," shouted

Linnea, as she pulled off the daisy's last petal, "It's Anthropus." She sighed. "Sequanna has favored us with a good omen. I shall carry daisies to the dance of Beltane."

"And I shall carry the woodland violets," said Boudicca. "And what hues will our tunics be?" she asked.

"Mine shall be the bright yellow of the heather and the gorse," said Linnea.

"And mine," said Boudicca, "shall be the soft purple of the wild hyacinth, the green of the woodland ivy, and the gold of the meadow buttercup. I must ask Mattilia to begin weaving today," she sighed. "And, we must prepare our offerings to secure the blessings of Sequanna. Richly scented petals from the woodland rose, wheat cakes to appease her great hunger, and animals carved from the sycamore which surrounds us in abundance to symbolize the blessing of bounty."

Boudicca peered at the sun lowering in the sky. "I must hurry to return before sundown," she said, throwing her arms about her friend as she rose to leave.

Linnea returned the embrace, looking wistfully at Boudicca, and looked out over the flocks of cowslips, daffodils and heather. Her idle time at an end, she must return to the chores of the farmer's daughter. Plowing the field, rocking the cradle, baking the bread, and spinning the flax. She rose to leave as well, startling the sunning frog into the waters below. Her burst of tinkling laughter echoed off the river's grassy banks.

As Boudicca made her way up the steep hillside below the gates of the city, she was thrown suddenly off balance by the rumbling of horses' hooves. There, on the road above her, the iron gates of the city flung back, was the Silures retinue, headed through the entrance of the stone and timber wall. And at the head of the procession, along with Cunobelinus, were the two young princes. Caractacus had added a full-blown mustache to his noble demeanor. But, it was Venutius who drew her attention. Tall astride his horse, his once slender body now bore the build of a Celtic warrior and his face, also mustachioed and once reflective only of the cares of youth, more somber.

Chapter Two

Boudicca scoured the handsome chest which took up the better part of a wall in her private chambers for a suitable tunic. Carved from the rich, red wood of the wild cherry tree, and covered with the carefully chiseled, elegant scrolls of a dedicated artisan, maidens with amber eyes dancing amidst them, and delicately-placed polished coral dredged up from the sea, it held tunics of every hue and texture known to the Celtic world. Heavy woolens woven from the shards of wool surrendered from the backs of sheep once a year to ward off the chill of the British winter. Linens the hue of the meadow buttercup and the riverbank hyacinth, carefully woven to offset the strength of the flax from whence it came, so carefully tended in the fields of the Celtic farmer. And even silk, dyed in the bright hues of the Far East and exchanged long ago on the Continent for the unpolished coral of the sea.

Boudicca chose a deep, green linen, bordered with the golden thread of a skilled, Coritani seamstress. To fasten the tunic at her left shoulder, a bronze fibula sculpted with the head of a dog, sporting a tiny coral eye. She chose as well a thick, golden torque, fashioned with the head of the sacred goose, and armlet to match.

16

And, to keep her feet from the hard clay floors of the palace's great hall, her softest pair of sandals, made from the hides of the game animals brought down by the palace's huntsmen.

As the chatter of the guests and servants rose in the hallway at the anticipation of so grand a feast, Mattilia arrived to dress Boudicca's long, red tresses to match the significance of the evening's event. Winding the strands of her thick, long locks into the shape of a rope worthy of a Celtic seaman, she piled and wound the length atop her head, securing the creation with amber-studded combs, and leaving the remainder to dangle in curls beyond her shoulders.

"Oh, Mattilia, it's beautiful," she said, as she studied her image in the scrolled, bronze looking glass the servant held before her face. "I must hurry to arrive before our guests," she said, as she threw her arms about Mattilia and scampered off in the direction of the great hall. As she rounded the corner that led away from the maze of corridors to the main hall, she slowed her pace to a dignified stroll. Mama would expect her to set an example of royal decorum.

Boudicca had just slipped through the entrance of the great hall when Catrinellia approached her. Dressed in a long, red tunic, with a torque depicting the hunt of the goddess Danu, her blond locks mingling with grey secured atop her head with two golden amber-studded combs, she presented the picture of royal presence she had long ago trained for. She put her hands on Boudicca's shoulders, and stood back to survey her.

Beaming, she announced, "Mattilia has outdone herself."

Reluctant to lose her edge, she continued. "Boudicca," she announced, "you must sit next to your father at the long, main banquet table. I shall be at his right hand and you must place yourself at his left. And, at your other side," she added, "must sit Mandorix and the two young sons of your father's brother Andromus. We must present our guests with a picture of tribal strength."

As princess to an ancient tribe losing numbers from the attacks of warring bands and tribal disputes, Boudicca would be wed to a wealthier and more powerful chieftain than Votorix if a suitable alliance could be found to strengthen the Coritani. But, it was to Mandorix that the weight of the Coritani throne would fall. Under Catrinellia's direction, Mandorix received training befitting a royal heir. He joined Votorix often in the hunt and accompanied him to affairs of state.

But, to Boudicca, Mandorix was a presence to be reckoned with. Though he often showed the stateliness of a youth beyond his years, he just as often chased her about the palace halls, begging her for a game of hide the boar's tooth or tag and run. Though she sometimes tried to interest him in more serious pursuits, his tumbling about brought giggles to her otherwise sober countenance.

As Boudicca made ready to answer Catrinellia, the high-pitched sounds of the horns that heralded the guests' arrival threw a hush over the chatter of the already assembled crowd, stopping gossip in mid-sentence of nobles and ladies-in-waiting alike. Heads turned to the entrance, where stood Cunobelinus, in a tunic of many colors and trousers dark in hue, a golden, coral-studded scabbard which depicted the feats of warriors from centuries past hitched to his waist. Flanking him stood Caractacus and Venutius, their own enameled scabbards and sword hilts depicting the valor of the Celtic battle.

As the guests were ushered to the table set aside for the Silures retinue, Votorix took his seat at the long table set aside for the Coritani royalty and nobility, and his top, military advisors. "Cunobelinus and his Silures retinue are welcome," he announced. "It is an honor to share our bounty with so valiant and noble a tribe." At his signal, servants brought platters heaped with roasted game to the tables, and flagons of wine, brought back from the Continent, and ale, fermented by palace hands, began to make their rounds.

Game birds abounded. The wild pigeon, the tiny sparrow, the meadow pheasant. The aroma of wild boar roasting on the spits over an open fire filled the air. The course flesh of the woodland stag, felled by the palace huntsmen. Fresh fish from the sea and the River Devon took their places on large, silver platters gleaming from the light of torches surrounding the great hall. Joints of mutton and beef from the carefully tended flocks of the Coritani farmer. Course, thick, bread turned out from the rye of the fields which stretched below the city's gates. And, of course, the delicate honey cakes turned out by the palace bakers and the soft, white cheese fermented in the crude creameries of the goatherd.

As subjects of a tribe which by necessity measured its stores, the Coritani nobles were determined to enjoy the rare dip into the palace larder to its fullest. To this end, they piled their plates with gusto, drank deep from the flagons of wine and ale which made their rounds, and caught up on the gossip left unattended by the labor of daily affairs. To Mandorix and the two young sons of Andromus, the event was a chance to play tag and run beneath the tables and around the hassocks, amidst a sea of noble legs, coaxed out only with the promise of tales to come.

And, minstrels dressed in muted hues made their way among the tables, tantalizing the ear with the strains of the harp and lyre.

"Mama," asked Boudicca, as she left the succulence of the wild, roast boar upon her plate and turned to Catrinellia, "when will we hear the stories of long ago?"

"When your father summons the bards and vates to appear before us," answered Catrinellia, licking her fingers sticky from the leg of a honey-glazed game bird.

Boudicca turned to Votorix who was lost in conversation with one of his top advisors. "Papa," she said, gently tugging on the sleeve of his tunic.

Votorix finished his sentence and turned toward her. "Boudicca," he said, as he lifted a large joint of meat from his plate, "what is so important to interrupt such a fine feast?"

"Papa, when will you summon the bards and vates to sing us the stories of the feats of our ancestors?" she asked.

"Boudicca," he answered, "it is proper to wait until our guests are served and acquainted with our great hall and the nobles of our tribe. But, the Silures look easy with ale and talk. I will summon Aladon to begin." Votorix gave the signal, causing nerves to give way in the vestibule where the bards and vates awaited their summons patiently to appear before him.

"Sire," spoke Aladon, who led the delegation as the chieftain's favorite, bowing deeply, "I beg leave to sing the stories of our ancestors."

"I give you permission to unfold your tale," answered Votorix. "But, you must please us with their deeds of valor."

Aladon bowed again, motioning the minstrels to come forth to support his tales with the soft strains of their harps and lyres.

I sing of Tuisto the earth-born god
Whose seed brought Mannus and his seed brought three
sons who gave their names to three tribes
entrenched along the Danube and the Rhine and along the
swamps and hills of the Hercynian forest onto the
plains and out into the sea.

The Chatti dwell in the Hycernian forest,
Which like a nursemaid guides them through its hills to
set them down on the edge of plains,
They rely not on fortune but on valor.
Pledging to the gods to stay unshorn their long, red
locks
Until a stand of courage release them from their
pledge.

Hardy in body, well-knit of limb, and fleet of mind,
Their battle plan as skillful as their Roman foes.
Their fiercest warriors stand first, marked by an iron
ring and gaze as fierce in peace as battle,
Their steady advance a terror to their foes.
Their women in battle to nurse and count their wounds,
To prod them with visions of the slavery of daughters,
wives, and sisters,
Their fiercest warriors' keep a burden to the choicest
tribal hosts.

The Chauci dwell along the bank of the Rhine,
Excelling in horsemanship where the Chatti excel on
foot,
The noblest of the land,
They dwell in peace and quiet, untouched by greed,
Yet, every man with arms ready at hand to raise in time
of need.

The Suebi live out at sea,
And in their sacred groves they worship mother earth,
the goddess Nerthus,
Who drives among them in her chariot drawn by cows,
bringing peace only with her presence,
and, when she withdraws, a return to battle.
Their battle dress a topknot erect upon their heads,
Their bodies dyed, their battles fought in the pitch of
the darkest night.

These be our ancestors,
Raised with free will and harmony of rank,
Unwashed, unclothed and nursed only by their mother,
Until the spirit of valor claims them as its own.
Driven to battle with neighbors, lured by booty, or by
envy of special favors of the gods, or by domineering
pride.
But, for two centuries plus ten,
They stood against the Roman foe
to lay claim to their freedom
with strength greater than all Gaul,
With energy greater than the peoples of the east

held in chains by despots.

The banquet guests stamped their feet and clapped their hands at the words of Aladon. "Aladon," begged Boudicca, shouting to rise above the raucous laughter of the guests and the noisy stomping of their approval of the bard's tales, "tell us the story of Dumnorix the Aeduan."

Aladon wiped the sweat from his brow, smiled, and bowed a low, sweeping bow in her direction. "I dedicate the tale of Dumnorix the Aeduan to the princess Boudicca," he said, straightening, the smile softening a face taut with nerves.

I sing of Dumnorix the Aeduan,
Brother to Divitiacus the Aeduan king,
A figure in the glory of all Gaul
Who a hundred years past gave aid to the Helveti
His wife's tribe, the fiercest in the land,
To flee the Roman foe or stand against it.

Several times did Dumnorix foil the Roman foe
Once, to keep grain from Roman armies
Another, to turn the Aeduan masses
Against the Roman foe,
Saved by his brother Divitiacus
A king turned loyal to the Roman armies and its gods.

As Gaul fell the Romans made Dumnorix hostage,
To sail with Caesar for our isle and battle,
But, the Aeduan chief ran from his Roman captors
To resist their pleas for return.

Dumnorix the Aeduan was felled with shouts
Urging on his followers.
'I am a free man.
I belong to a free country.'

The guests again stomped their feet in approval of Aladon's tale. But, despite the gentle strains of the minstrel's harps and lyres, the headiness of the wine and ale from flagons so generously passed round began to take its toll. Challenges from duels of the sword to dice began to make the rounds, often cut short by the sudden loud snores of one or another participant. But, a collective gasp arose as Galorix, son of the highborn noble Mandelamus, and newly risen from the dance of spears to honor Cocidius, god of the battle, rose to prove the valor in his newly pledged manhood.

Striding across the clay floor of the great hall, slightly tipsy from deep draughts of ale, his muscles rippled as he pulled a long, bronze sword, a gift from the rites of Cocidius, from an elaborately enameled scabbard. As he reached the Silures table, he strode toward Caractacus. The Silures prince sat erect, moving little muscle nor lowering his gaze, but silencing his talk with the Silures nobles.

The young noble tapped Caractacus' shoulder with the tip of his sword as he stood before him. "Silures prince," he began, his voice working carefully to form the words with a tongue slightly thick with ale, "I Galorix, son of Mandelamus, challenge you to a duel of valor." He continued, "I prove the strength of a small but honorable tribe."

Caractacus arose to face Galorix. He knew that to fight this youth to victory would pull a promising warrior from the ranks of his hosts. But, to turn away from a challenge would just as surely show cowardice. "I accept your challenge," he said, as he pulled his sword from its scabbard, carefully hitched to the links of gold which belted his ochre tunic.

Caractacus and Galorix stood to face each other, their swords at the ready, tips facing upwards toward the height of the great hall ceiling. A roar went up from the crowd as Votorix gave a signal to begin.

The sounds of swords clashing filled the room and cheers went up as one or another of the duelers gained an advantage. Boudicca gasped as the two evenly matched in body grappled to gain a thrust of the sword. But, despite the even match of build, Galorix' youth and headiness of ale took its toll, giving way for Caractacus to the many seasons of feigned sparring in the halls of the Silures palace and the deftness of his ways in the woodland hunt. With one carefully placed blow, he knocked the bronze sword from his opponent's hand, blocking his path to lift it once again. Galorix stood firm, ready to receive the final blow in a match fairly fought.

Caractacus threw his sword down upon the floor of the great hall. "You have fought well, Galorix", he said. "You will make a fine warrior if hordes threaten the walls of the Coritani. But, we have come not to take the lives of the Coritani, but to align ourselves with them. I look forward to your place at your father's elbow in council tomorrow with the sunrise."

As Galorix returned his sword to its scabbard and made his way back to the side of Mandelamus, the noise of the crowd rose, mingling with shouts and laughter, buoyed by the excitement of the joust and the pleasures of vineyard and alehouse. The guests began to rise, sated with the pleasures of the table, and the merriment of highborn nobles, trained in the judgments of civil order, and the military advisors, toughened from the field of battle, filled the room. Boudicca broke from her appointed place at table, making her way as quickly as possible around the knots of laughing nobles and servants tidying the remains of the palace larder toward the Silures table. As she reached Caractacus, she threw her arms about him.

"Oh, Caractacus," she said, feeling easier to have her childhood friend under the touch of her arms, "I was so worried that you would be run through by Galorix with the sword he received at Sanheim."

"Why, Boudicca," he said, smiling down at her as he put his arms about her to return the greeting, "you know it takes more than a young noble fresh from the dance of Cocidius to fell a Silures prince. My great-grandfather Litaviccus stood against the Romans."

"So Diviticus relates in his tales of our island," she returned. "But, you must help me choose the mistletoe for my first bonfire dance at Beltane. Only you and Venutius are suited to such a task."

"It will be an honor to consider the quest the first task of our visit following our debate at council," he said, solemnly. "But, you must ask Venutius yourself," he said, as he turned to the Iberian prince, quietly waiting to greet her.

"Oh, Venutius," she said, throwing her arms about him as she realized she had ignored him in her concern for Caractacus, "I must show you how straight my arrows fly from the bows you taught me to carve."

"I am anxious to watch their flight," he said, laughing gently, "and I will help to choose the glossiest leaves of the mistletoe vine to lay upon the crown of your tresses come Beltane."

At this moment, Cunobelinus intercepted with the warning that the Silures, worn from hard travel, must repair to their bedchambers to insure fresh thoughts for the council meeting.

Boudicca took her leave of Caractacus and Venutius, throwing her arms about them once again, with promises of their woodland jaunt to keep her.

As she headed toward her bedchamber to exchange her evening finery for her nightclothes, she devised stories of hobgoblins and dragons as she went. She knew Mandorix would creep to her bedchamber as soon as the last candle was snuffed, awake from the excitement of guests roaming the palace halls, to beg a story of Sanheim, his most favorite of festivals, and to snuggle beneath her quilts for a moment's peace from the royal regimen. She searched the palace halls for Mattilia to unwind her long, red tresses.

Chapter Three

Sunlight streamed into the council hall of the Coritani palace. The Silures, refreshed from the hospitality of the rude but comfortable palace bedchambers generously piled high with the soft skins of woodland animals, took their places on the straw hassocks set about in groups, nobles interspersed with warriors retired from battle, scarred from the skirmishes of the past, but sharp with the knowledge of the battlefield. The Coritani assembled as well, sober with thought but lightening the moment for their guests with a well-placed pleasantry or two. Cunobelinus, splendid in partial military garb, sat in the center, flanked by Caractacus and Venutius. Votorix sat opposite. As tribal host chieftain, he began.

"We welcome the Silures," he said, in his richest and most ceremonial tones, "in gratitude for their journey away from the daily cares of their tribe to talk of alliance in protection of both the Silures and the Coritani. The Silures stand strong in numbers along the western coast of our island, ten to our one. But, the Coritani stand strong in honor, as do the Silures, and in our place in the north at the southernmost tip of the wildest and most uninhabited stretches of our island." He paused to let his conciliatory but honest assessment of their respective positions take hold.

He continued. "Our tribal cities have long been beset by forays from the fierce Belgae of the south, great in numbers and led by Cassivellaunus, depleting our warriors and deflecting our energies from the daily affairs of bringing grain from our fields, coral and fish from the sea, and turning our copper to pots on our blacksmith's forges, toward the building and repairing of our timber walls, trenches, and bulwarks."

"But," he added, "the Belgae do not send all their warriors to destroy our fields and cities at once. They attack the great Trinobantes tribe as well with great force, and conduct raids upon the harvest of the smaller Segontiaci and Bibroci tribes. But, we must live in fear of an all-out campaign. The Belgae covet the coral we pull from the sea, and the thick woods and heavy marshes of our lands, so superior for the defense of battle for so warlike a tribe."

Votorix, ending his discourse on the military position of the Coritani, leaned back slightly on his hassock, leaving silence for thought and awaiting a reply from the Silures. Cunobelinus shifted slightly on his hassock and spoke carefully. "Although the Silures sustain the occasional ransack of foraging tribes upon our tribal fields, our numbers and the use to which we have put our strength to let no enemy gain advantage has kept us from the attack of even the largest of our island tribes. But, we must keep our military always at the ready, with large numbers of chariots, swords, and helmets fashioned and in good repair. Your tribal lands are thick with timber and your earth with copper for our bronze. We must keep these safe for trade."

As Cunobelinus finished pouring forth the Silures position, he paused, awaiting the thoughts of his nobles. Andromatus, the highest born of the Silures contingent, weathered with age and the weight of many decisions, spoke first. "It is within our interests to protect the bounty which shores up our waiting warriors. But, we must not deplete our forces on a ready basis."

The Silures noble Mandolatus spoke next. "We must shore up trade with the Coritani to stay the Belgae from a foothold in the north. A greater trade will give more bounty to our northern neighbors to draw into their forces the warriors of the Danube and the Rhine who fight only with the promise of bounty before the battle."

Andromatus spoke again. "It is also within our interest to come to the rescue of a tribe friendly to peace and trade, if besieged by so warlike a band. If the Coritani cities are besieged by the Belgae, our farmers must drop their plows and our merchants their trade, to send warriors to the aid of our northern neighbors. But, if we are to ally our tribes, we must extract full military prowess from the Coritani as well. What say you ancient warriors of the battlefield?"

Andromatus shifted on his hassock as he looked among the Silures grouped about him, searching out the warriors, past their prime in the hand-to-hand conflicts of the battlefield but versed well in the strategies of battle. A murmuring arose as thoughts pondering the strengths of the Coritani passed round. The warrior Gatorix, his shaggy blond hair turned almost grey, his body adorned with the numerous scars of his many conflicts, which he displayed with pride as signs of his superior courage and prowess on the battlefield among his peers, spoke first. "The Silures rely on the great courage of their warriors and the strength of their numbers to repel an enemy. The Coritani, while small in numbers and brave on the battlefield, employ great tactical skills to outwit their enemy. We could make use of such skills in our skirmishes. Where to approach an enemy, how to approach them, when to come upon them, and how to steer a battle to gain the advantage."

Domorix, a warrior long retired but still with keen interest in battle, spoke next. "And, in the case of all-out attack upon the Silures, we must extract a promise from the Coritani to send their warriors in full force to the aid of our struggle."

Cunobelinus leaned toward Votorix. "Our nobles and warriors put forth thoughts for you to ponder. What say you to their terms?"

"I must consult with the nobles and warriors of the Coritani before I give an answer," said Votorix, turning to the groups assembled about him. He turned back, addressing the Silures. "Perhaps," he said, "we might stroll in the air and the sunlight about the palace to ponder the weight of the terms you have put before us." He rose, gathering his advisors about him to lead the way through the narrow, winding halls of the palace through a side door, hewn heavy and thick from the woodland ash, to the grounds beyond, a luxury set aside for the royal palace alone among the timber, clay and daub, thatched-roof dwellings huddled side-by-side inside the high, stone and timber walls of the hilltop city.

Votorix stepped out upon the wild grasses of the palace grounds, kept low by the scythes of the palace groundskeepers, paths marked by the rough-hewn stones of the palace quarries, overlooking the stretches of Coritani fields, the sprouts of the grain from seeds sown by the farmer's hand rising plentifully below. A nightingale perched upon the branch of a wild cherry tree heavy with the blossoms of spring burst into song.

Votorix, caught up by conversation with a group of Coritani nobles, broke from his place among them to move alongside Cunobelinus, whose noble carriage, though slightly stooped by the mark of seasons passed, was unbroken by tribal strife. Votorix, whose large frame topped by long blond locks, nearly untarnished by grey, mirrored the strength of his youth, slowed his gait to match the pace of the Silures chief. "Cunobelinus," he said, "you have served the Silures well and with the honor of your father and grandfather. Your tribe fares well. It flows with bounty and endures prosperity and peace. But, you must tire with the weight of tribal guidance."

Cunobelinus turned to Votorix, his grey locks thinned from the passing years and the strife of affairs of state, but flowing as in youth. "Our people bring grain from the earth, husband great numbers of cattle and herd great flocks of sheep, bring pearls from the sea for trade, and worship our gods from sunrise to sunrise in freedom. It pleases me to serve my tribe long and in good health, to don my ceremonial garb to see Beltane come and Sanheim go with the greater and greater bounty of the gods. But, I tire with the weight of affairs of state. With the aid of the Druids, justice is served and inter-tribal peace enacted. But, the pettiness of the nobles, the demands of the merchants over the arteries of trade and commerce, and the demands of the military to maintain the peace of our tribal nation, arise with every sunrise. I look forward to the thoughts of youth to spur the tribe and carry it onward."

"You have two fine youths to carry the Silures forward," said Votorix, glancing at Caractacus and Venutius, lost in conversation with a group of young nobles ahead. "Caractacus grows strong and fine in limb since last he stood upon the soil of our city. And, Venutius has filled out his slender Iberian frame."

"Caractacus has been trained in the most noble of pursuits," said Cunobelinus. "Andromatus has spent many seasons teaching him the gentility of the nobles, our palace huntsmen the intricacies of the woodland hunt, Gatorix the strategies of the battlefield, and our Druids devotion to the gods. And, he has been at my elbow at every tribal council.

But, despite his training," he continued, "Caractacus is yet most comfortable alone with his thoughts on the woodland hunt. He cares little for the trappings of leadership, prizing the farmers' meals of bread and cheese taken on skins upon the floors of their simple, clay huts and served by their children the same as the feast of a noble's quarters."

"And, Venutius, how does he fare since you brought him from the shores of Iberia and the protection of his father Erithrominus?" asked Votorix.

"Venutius takes well to royal training," said Cunobelinus, "and works hard to please. He is skilled in the hunt and works well with the nobles, urging them to settle their differences in land ownership with as few petty squabbles as possible. He will make a fine prince consort, carrying the word of the Silures to another mighty tribe of our island, with the hope to bind our two tribes in trade and in peace."

"And you, Votorix," said Cunobelinus, "how go your royal heirs?"

"Mandorix is young, yet," said Votorix, "but he studies well the royal ways. He accompanies me on the hunt and sits often in council. But, he has yet to study the ways of eloquence, justice, and devotion at the hand of our Druid Diviticus or learn the order of the lands from our nobles or the ways of commerce from our tradesmen."

"But, Boudicca," he continued, his face alit with thoughts of his eldest heir, born red-faced and squalling, with a tuft of red locks upon her head, an event which had never dimmed in her father's memory despite the passing seasons, "grows from a creature happiest in the fields and woodlands in childhood to learning a devotion to tribal ways. Boudicca joins the maiden's dance come Beltane, and will make a fine queen to a chieftain of a larger and more powerful tribe, to revive the ancient power of the Coritani."

Ahead, the laughter of the two young princes and a knot of young nobles broke the thoughts of the two kings strolling along the stone-cut paths and interrupted the arguments of the nobles and warriors on the details of tribal agreement. Spurred by the fresh air of the palace grounds and the mid-morning sunshine, the talk of Caractacus, Venutius, and the young nobles of both tribes had soon left the plane of tribal agreements and military disputes for the newly awakened fascinations of youth. Duels to the finish after a gala feast, contests of the dice turned spellbound by a youthful future in the balance, and the newly discovered charms of Celtic maidens once their playmates in the fields and woodlands of the British countryside.

Ambigetorix, son of Andromatus, was entertaining them with a tale of his narrow escape from the loss of all his lands as heir to the highest-born noble of the Silures and promise of a ten season servitude as sheepherder to Manolinius, son of a nearby noble, in a contest of dice, so determined was he to win. But, Andromatus, keeping company with a group of elder statesmen not far from the ill-fated gaming table, turned to amble over as onlooker, a look upon his face which reflected long seasons upon the battlefield in the service of the Silures and in the council halls of kings. Ambigetorix, with his back to his father, heeded not the elder noble's stern look, but Manolinius, nerves taut with intensity in the promise of gaining the servitude of a childhood rival, answered the look with a nervous twitch of his elbow, sending the dice sprawling to the floor to default the match. The roar that went up from the crowd of onlookers signaled an end to the contest.

Next, Alonius, anxious to turn the talk to the emerging charms of Celtic maidens, turned toward Caractacus, his friend since childhood. "Caractacus," he said, a look of gentle teasing passing over his features, sprung from the closeness of childhood, "you look at the maiden Cortitiana with the eyes of a bull in the field. But, she is the daughter of a Silures noble. Perhaps it will be necessary to take as your queen the daughter of a tribal chieftain, to bind the tribe to the Silures in added strength."

Caractacus turned to Alonius, a serious look replacing his former mirth. "I have spoken to Father," he said, "of his plans for me to wed. The Silures are a powerful tribe, great in numbers. To align with another tribe through marriage would add only numbers, not strength. The Silures in council hold to keep loyalty within our tribe to be of more import in strength than to align with another."

A look of resolve passed over his face, accompanied by the dreaminess of youth. "Cortitiana and I have been playmates since childhood," he said. "We have marveled at the croaking frog of the marshes, slid the banks of the Avon River wetting our cloaks in the chill of winter, and stood together as the sun rose over our ancient grove. It is fitting that we should spend our lives together in the service of the Silures."

As the young nobles turned their thoughts to speculating which Celtic maiden might grace the hearths of their futures, and the young Silures pondered the impact of the proposed royal marriage upon their tribal status, Votorix strode alongside, his serious countenance banishing all thought of further jabs at the young romantic, and signaling a return to the purpose of their gathering. "We must go again inside the council hall," he said. "You have ridden long and hard to the gates of our city. We must continue our talk of differences to strike agreement which will strengthen our tribes in seasons to come."

Votorix again led the way through the palace's winding halls to the council hall, settling himself upon the same hassock as before, as did the nobles and warriors of each of the two tribes. Votolanus, a high born Coritani noble, spoke first. "I agree with Mandolatus to increase the trade between our two tribes, though distance separates us. We must get to you the copper of our earth and the timber our lands grow to strengthen your bulwarks, your chariots, and your warrior's sword. And, we must bring from you the pearls you pull from the sea to enhance our artisans' wares and the swords, spears, and scabbards you turn on your craftsmens' forges."

"To liven the trade between our two tribes will increase our bounty," he continued, shifting his weight slightly upon his hassock and leaning forward as a look of greater intensity crossed his face, "a sign of strength to repel the Belgae intruders. But, I do not agree with Mandolatus to call first the warriors of the Danube and the Rhine if the Belgae make attack upon our city, but to call Silures warriors to strengthen our defense in battle."

Ordovetorix, a Coritani noble advanced in years and veteran of the field of battle, with a voice still marked by the volume and depth of youth, spoke next. "I agree with Votolanus," he said, his thundering voice filling the room as he sat erect upon his hassock. "The warriors of the Danube and the Rhine fight fiercely and with great courage. But, they fight for bounty, to prove their courage and to save their hides. They care not to stay the Belgae from our island's tribal gates."

"But, the Silures," he continued, "have an interest to stay the Belgae from overrunning our isle and to keep the peace among our Celtic tribes. They must be first to strengthen our numbers on the field of battle if the Belgae make attack upon the gates of our city." His thoughts put forth, Ordovetorix leaned back his frame, still ample despite the withering flesh which hung upon it, upon his hassock.

Silence filled the room as nobles and warriors of both tribes juggled the terms put forth against the advantages of their tribal pursuits. Votorix spoke, addressing the Silures contingent. "How do you answer our terms? We must bring forth an agreement suitable to both our tribes."

After careful thought, and some shifting upon his hassock, Caractacus spoke. "If we are to keep our tribal cities free from the attack of raiders we must be prepared to add our warriors to your numbers in case of a Belgae attack upon your tribal city. If the Silures are attacked, or our fields foraged, we will take in exchange the advice of your warriors upon the field of battle."

Venutius, silent but thoughtful until now, spoke next. "To increase the trade between us would add to the bounty of both our tribes. It would as well perhaps increase the power of our trade upon the Continent, the fine wines of the vineyards of Gaul, the oils and scents of Iberia, and the silks they take in trade on journeys far to the east."

"A lively trade," he continued, "will keep our merchants and nobles busy and prosperous, our warriors from longing too often for the field of battle, and discourse flowing between us."

Cunobelinus, listening quietly as Caractacus and Venutius put forth their thoughts, spoke next. "I agree with the two princes of my household," he said. "Trade will strengthen our tribes and the knowledge of your warriors our position on the battlefield. We must pledge to aid your tribe in the protection from raiders of the south. We must also enlist your aid should raiders threaten our tribal gates."

Votorix turned to the Coritani nobles and warriors grouped about him. "Does the Coritani council," he asked, "agree to the terms of our distant neighbors who have generously agreed to ride to sit in council with us under our roof?"

The Coritani advisors nodded their assent, one by one, as Votorix's glance passed among them. Votorix addressed Cunobelinus. "We pledge to assist you in time of attack upon your cities' gates. We also pledge to send emissaries to talk of increased trade between our tribes."

Votorix then turned to both groups. "It is rare that we sit together under one roof," he said. "Perhaps there are thoughts which you desire to put forth about our life upon this isle."

Immediately, a murmuring arose among both the Coritani and the Silures, rising almost abruptly in intensity. Andromatus spoke, his tone weighted with the concern of the political intricacies of councils past, silencing the murmuring about him. "There have been rumblings among our Druids," he said, "of a concern that

Rome now wants to subdue our entire isle. They fear attack upon our shores."

Mandolatus spoke next. "Our nobles fear the greed of Rome as well. In their travels upon the Continent in behalf of the commerce of the vessels of our artisans and the pearls we pull from the sea, which the Romans covet, they hear talk that Rome must again satisfy its hunger to subdue. The threat of uprisings in Gaul and Iberia long gone, the Celts live there as Romans. The Celts of Germania defend as strongly as the Romans attack the lands beyond the Danube and the Rhine, wearing after more than two centuries the patience, military supplies, and numbers of both."

"There is talk," he continued, his voice rising in intensity, "that the Romans look beyond the Continent to our shores to finish Caesar's attack of nearly a century ago. It is said that the tribute promised Caesar by five of our isle's tribes, which they often forget to pay, is no longer enough to satisfy the coffers of Rome, or the lands it occupies enough to satisfy its glory and its power. And," he added, "Rome does not forget our aid to our Gallic neighbors in their defense against its armies."

Votorix addressed the council next, pausing to pull together his thoughts. "If Rome attacks our shores, we will align ourselves with larger tribes east of our gates. Prasutagus of the Iceni rules a tribe large in numbers and rich in wealth. He negotiates with neighboring tribes to enjoy a reign of peace and compromise. His emissaries are trained long and well in the art of diplomacy."

"We have not numbers to spare," he continued. "We will attempt to maintain our way of life through diplomacy with the Romans."

Cunobelinus spoke next. "We will meet the Romans only on the battlefield," he said, speaking evenly as he sat straight upon his hassock. "We will not surrender, for if we surrender our swords we surrender our spirits as well. Under the armies of my grandfather Curnovitrix the Silures repelled the Roman armies and drove them from our tribal lands, to leave our island with no Silures bounty upon their ships, nor promise of Silures tribute upon their lips. If they climb again upon the shores of our island to attack the gates of our cities or the fields of our tribal lands, we will carry out our heritage again upon the field of battle."

Domitatus, a Coritani noble trained in the art of commerce and the battlefield, spoke up. "In many lands upon the Continent, Celtic tribes live side by side with Roman governors and armies."

At this, Venutius, listening patiently to both sides speak, spoke up, barely able to contain an anger honed in a land dominated for a over a century by Roman rule, reducing the power of Celtic tribal chieftains like his father to a distant memory, rarely recounted any longer around an evening fire. "It is true that many Celts upon the Continent enjoy the life of Rome. Gone are the huts that for centuries sheltered Celts in Gaul and in Iberia, replaced by grand stone villas with courtyards and even Roman baths. Gone are the dirt paths trod hard upon by the horses of Celtic merchants in search of trade, of royal messengers and huntsmen, and by the feet of our farmers in search of a hare for an evening's supper. In their place are roads paved with the stone of our countryside and the sun-dried clay of our earth, connecting our towns and dwellings in grand design. And gone are the skins and the furs that once covered our bodies against the chill of winter, replaced by the toga of Rome."

"But," he continued, "the nobles grow fat and lazy around the table in the service of the Roman governors. And, the farmers, once toiling for the defense of their own tribal lands and the taste of cheese and bread upon their supper plate after a long day's work in the field, now taxed higher and higher as the seasons pass, toil as well for the richness of the Roman table, where no expense is spared to lay upon it delicacies imported from the farthest reaches of lands, the revelry of Roman entertainments and games, and the attempts to conquer their own ancestral tribes across the Rhine."

"The artisans," he added, "no longer valued for their craft, are put to work to pave the roads and raise the Roman villas. Celtic men, once brothers of chieftains, nobles, or merchants, all warriors of the field, are taken to pull the salt from Roman mines or fill the gladiator ring to quicken Roman pleasure. Their women are sent to fill the urns and tote the scents of highborn Roman women."

"And," he added, as he hunched forward, his tones more hushed, "there are no Druids to prepare the rituals of our ancestors in our prayers to Belenus for the rains of harvest, to instruct us in the signs of a telltale omen, to administer justice when our own tempers have gone astray, and to offer the words of wisdom. Gone are the bonfires of Sanheim and the sound of the clashing swords as our youth make a pact of manhood. Gone are the flowers of Beltane strewn before the image of Sequanna at its maidens' dance. Gone are the Celtic gods. Instead," he said, pausing to catch breath, "the Celts must worship Roman gods and build, with their own hands and at their own expense, temples to the Roman Emperor Tiberius." At this, Venutius leaned back, himself surprised at so lengthy a rush of thoughts from a youth so often spare with words.

Votorix spoke next, pausing to let the murmuring which arose, subside, as nobles disagreed with nobles and warriors uttered battle cries in a show of strength. "We must end our council as the sun begins to set," he said. "We have made agreement to protect our tribes from the raiders of our island. We are not able to make agreement on the threat of attack from Rome. But, we Celts of this isle must listen to our neighbors of the Continent who hear the words of the Roman governors. If Roman armies sail for our shores, we must make haste to send warning to our friendly tribes, that they may prepare to meet the Romans before they lay waste our cities and our fields."

Votorix rose. "We thank our Silures guests," he said, "for riding to our gates to leave behind for even short a time the import of daily tribal affairs. We wish to offer you the comforts of our palace walls and of its grounds. The servants of our stable and our huntsmen welcome you in a grand hunt prepared in your honor for the morrow."

Cunobelinus also rose, still grand in stature despite the wearing of the day. "The Silures thank the Coritani," he returned, "for the comforts you have so generously poured forth. We look forward to riding at your side to chase the proud stag and clumsy boar of the Coritani forest."

Votorix led the way as the nobles and warriors of the two tribal groups strolled from the council hall to pursue the activities of evening. The young to chase the maidens, the gaming match, and the duel brought on by ale and the exuberance of youth. The old to satisfy the palate with the joys of table, to compare the ways of commerce and administration, and to duel with wagging tongues the exploits of seasons past.

As they reached the end of the hall which led from the council room to the start of the narrow, winding hallways which led to the palace's great hall, its courtyard, and its maze of private bedchambers set off to the side, the laughter and the gossip which flowed freely among them kept them from notice of the Coritani princess, who stood behind a large, stone column raised in support of the thatch of the palace roof. As the council had passed, Boudicca had surprised Catrinellia with her willingness as a student of royal duties, and Mandorix as a pretend pony on a grand and glorious hunt about the palace halls. As she searched the knots of passing nobles for Caractacus and Venutius, she wondered who would find the glossiest length of mistletoe to crown her tresses come Beltane in their search of the sacred grove on the morrow.

Chapter Four

Boudicca awoke with the first rays of the early morning sun. She longed to rush to the Silures quarters to awaken Caractacus and Venutius, but she knew it would not be proper. Instead, she arose and pulled from her great, cherry wood chest a favorite tunic in hues of the darkest woodland greens, and a woolen cloak to match, to guard against the chill of the early morn. She added to it a pair of sandals turned from the toughest of boar hides, and a pair of her sturdiest trousers, for she knew Caractacus and Venutius would wish to ride the plains of the Coritani countryside and to explore the bogs, dried with the winds of winter and awaiting the rains of spring, and the great forests of their childhood visits along the way.

She splashed a bit of water, hauled from the Coritani countryside and held in a great earthenware pitcher along the wall of her bedchamber, quickly upon her face and hastily pulled a boar's bristle brush through the nighttime tangle of her long, red tresses. Then, she headed for the palace stables to choose a mount, detouring slightly to the great, palace kitchen, alit with the rays of the early morning sun, and noisy with the bustle of bakers turning the morning cakes of wheat to a golden brown, to leave word with the kitchen servants to pack her a meal ample enough to share with the two Silures princes.

As she trod the dimly lit hallways toward the bright sun of the outdoors, she thought of Tricerbantes, her mount since childhood. Papa had chosen him for her, an Albino small in stature and carefully bred and foaled from the most prized of the palace herds, born with the spirit of his ancestors of the wild. As they trained in the shadow of the palace stables, under the watchful eye of the head stable servant, he would let only Boudicca climb upon his back, her chubby legs hanging about his sides. Together, with the passing seasons, they rode the Coritani countryside, often without benefit of saddle. But, now, Tricerbantes was old. She must give him rest, and choose a mount to keep pace with the steeds of Caractacus and Venutius, horses bred for the speed and stamina of the journey.

She pushed open the small, heavy, wooden door that led to the palace courtyard, and crossed its well-worn paths to the entranceway of the stable, its large, wooden doors flung open against the morning sun. As she crossed its threshold onto the clay floor, strewn with the wild, dried grasses of the countryside, she heard a familiar whinny arise from the farthest end of the stable. As long as she could remember, Tricerbantes had always acknowledged her presence. But, now, his whinny went up from a body which lay longer prone on a pile of hay. She raced among the early morning activity, a groom with a boar's bristle brush at work on the golden mane of a stallion, another feeding himself on legs more feeble with the passing seasons, and placed his nose over the stall door in greeting. Boudicca laughed as she stroked his muzzle.

"How goes it, Tricerbantes," she asked, as he returned a gentle whinny in answer.

She turned to see Belanus, the head stable servant, in attendance. "Belanus," she asked, "could I please Tricerbantes with the taste of honey?"

He turned in answer toward the stores of honey kept in earthenware pots stacked along the highest of the rough-hewn shelves of the stable. He returned, toting a large share upon an earthenware slab. She dipped her hand into the nectar and brought it up to Tricerbantes' mouth, a treat she had often used for work well done. He nibbled gently until the sweet liquid disappeared entirely from her hand. She laughed, and patted him upon his mane.

"You must rest, now, Tricerbantes," she said, as she stroked his soft white muzzle once again, "but we shall ride the plains again together."

She turned to Belanus. "What mount do you have ready for saddle to ride the countryside this morn?" she asked.

"I have just the mount to tend to an early morning frolic," he said, as she followed him to the stall of a dapple gray mare, frisky though she had not yet left the stable. "Will she fill your wishes, princess?" he asked, as he stood patiently by the mare, awaiting her answer.

"Oh, yes," she answered. "And, you must saddle the Silures princes' stallions as well," she added, "as we must leave as soon as they appear."

She moved aside to free the grooms to scurry about in the fulfillment of her request. As she stood, she felt a pair of hands, untouched by the roughness of the labor of the field or kiln, but toughened by sword and bow, encircle themselves about her eyes.

"Princess," said a voice, chuckling and deep with the energy of the morn, "you must guess which warriors have answered your quest of mistletoe for Beltane."

Boudicca giggled, as she feigned the silence of thought. "Perhaps it is Votan," she spoke, in reference to the image of a bold and courageous warrior of ancient Celtic myth. "Or," she paused, "perhaps it is two Silures princes who have at last decided to arise from their bedcovers to join a search for the glossiest of mistletoe that clings to the oak of the sacred grove."

She laughed as she flung Caractacus' great hands from about her eyes and turned to throw her arms about him. Then, she embraced Venutius, standing patiently by, silent but with eyes asparkle. As they stood, Belanus and his attendants arrived with their mounts, groomed and saddled, ready with the energy of hand-fed oats, and fresh from the rest of a stall ample with hay.

Boudicca and the two Silures princes rode their mounts slowly through the gates of the Coritani city onto the grassy slope of the hillside below. Caractacus, straight upon his horse, spoke first. "I shall race to the great forest beyond the sacred grove" he proposed, his deep laughter rumbling against the quiet of the hillside. "The last to arrive shall act as servant, spreading our meal beneath the shade of a woodland tree."

"I shall see that I arrive before you," answered Boudicca, raising the reins of her dapple grey in the palms of her hands.

"Never cast aside the speed of an Iberian prince," retorted Venutius, hunching forward upon his stallion to gain upon his two companions.

Caractacus sat tall in his saddle as he gave the command to begin. "Ready. Forward, ho!" he shouted, as he spurred his stallion onward, shouting on his companions' mounts as he went.

As the three sped down the hillside out upon the meadow, where daisies sprouted newly risen with the early morning rain, the wind rushed through Boudicca's long, red tresses. She laughed as she sped ahead, her dapple gray carrying her along to the great woodland beyond. As she approached its edge, the mounts of Caractacus and Venutius pulled alongside, their laughter mingling with the song of the willow wren among the sedge, and leaving in question a winner to their race. Caractacus declared himself their servant and toted their morning meal to the shade of a great sycamore tree, its clumps of yellow blossoms aburst with the spring, and its large, flowing branches a support to the nest of the willow wren upon its brown speckled eggs.

The three sat upon the dark, green linen cover Caractacus had spread along the roots of the sycamore, to take their meal of the soft, creamy cheese turned from the milk of the palace goatherd and ripened in its creamery, wheat cakes, and goat milk held cool in skins. As they sat, the song of the robin and the blackbird mingled with the rushing of the woodland streams and the faint scent of the pink and white anemones along the mossy floor. As they ate, they gazed upon the height of the trees, the blue of the sky visible only through the topmost branches, the sycamore, the oak, the cherry and the maple, grown awesome with the passing seasons.

Caractacus spoke first. "This forest must have been a great refuge for the warriors of our isle against the Roman armies," he said, as he leaned his body against the thickness of the sycamore trunk.

Boudicca spoke next. "Diviticus says warriors hid among the trees of the forest, to jump upon the Roman armies when they knew not. And, yonder bog would catch them," she added, "for

Roman warriors have no equal upon the Continent of the tangle of peat and grasses along the softness of the floor of our island bogs."

"The great trees of the forest provide refuge as well from the ravaging tribes of the south," said Venutius. "It would do well for the artisans of the Coritani to fell trees only from forests thinned already by nature or the axe."

"We must move on to the sacred grove," said Caractacus, as he began to pack up the remains of their morning meal. "Diviticus will await us."

"But, first, we must catch a fish for Diviticus' supper," said Venutius, as he lifted the green, linen cover from the foot of the sycamore tree. "I will race you to the banks of the Devon," he laughed, as he got a running start to jump upon the back of his stallion. Boudicca and Caractacus jumped upon their mounts as well, catching Venutius as he raced across the meadow, his laughter loud against the rush of his stallion through the tall grasses and the clap of his horse's hooves upon its sod.

The three reached the banks of the Devon together, dismounting to lash their horses to the sparse stand of trees which lined the top of the riverbank. Venutius headed downstream to catch a fish as offering for Diviticus' evening meal. And, Caractacus sprawled himself in the shade of a great sycamore tree, its trunk grown tall toward the sun, its roots spread wide to hold the earth of the riverbank.

Boudicca raced down the grassy slope, unfastening her cloak and dropping it as she went, to skip along the large stones of the river placed helter-skelter by nature not far from the grassy shore. As she skipped along the stones, made smooth and glossy by the rush of the river's waters, she lost her footing, sending her into the midst of the clear and sparkling water of the Devon. She rose laughing, making her way up the slope toward Caractacus, her wet tunic clinging to her body as she ran. Caractacus laughed in return, as she dropped down upon the grasses near him to wring the Devon's waters from her linen tunic and to dry herself in the warmth of the morning sun.

"Caractacus," asked Boudicca, shaking her tresses as she wrung the water from them, "will you join the hunt this day?"

"Yes, Boudicca," he answered, lifting himself slightly as he raised himself upon his elbow. "I bring down often the hare and the quail upon the Silures lands. But, our woods are sparse, making it difficult to stalk the wild boar and the woodland stag. I look forward to returning to the Silures with the salted meat of the boar and the smoked joints of the woodland stag."

"Then, I shall wait with Diviticus," she answered, "for he has promised to share with me the omens of the ancient Celtic rites."

As they sat, a wren in the sycamore singing its morning song, Venutius appeared, his tunic dripping the waters of the Devon. He smiled as he held fast to a speckled, brown trout, slippery and wiggling still between his hands. "This noble fish nearly left my grasp for upstream waters," he said. "But, now, it will fill Diviticus' plate as offering for his evening meal."

He threw the fish upon the grass as he sat, catching his breath from the chase of the trout as it darted to and fro among the rocks of the Devon. He gazed at the sparkling waters passing over the jagged rocks as they went. Then, he rose. "We must depart for the sacred grove," he said. "We promised a certain maiden we would join her in a quest for the glossiest mistletoe of the woodland. We must make haste before the prized of the vine is carried off by celebrants of Belanus."

The three made their way to the sacred grove, hitching their mounts to the ample trees along its edge. As they trod the paths that led to Diviticus' hut, the rays of the sun which lit their way were few, seeking openings among the treetops of the thickly wooded grove. As they reached the clearing which held Diviticus' hut, Boudicca burst forth through the brush to embrace the Druid, lost in the study of the omens of the grove, the tracks of a woodland hare, the song of a robin as it called out its morning song.

"I have brought Caractacus and Venutius," she said, as she threw her arms about him, catching her breath from her sudden sprint across the clearing. Diviticus turned toward the two princes as they strolled across the clearing, stretching his arms outward toward them. "Greetings, Diviticus," shouted Caractacus, as they moved their steps more quickly, embracing him as they met. "I bring you greetings from Orthoveterix," he added, delivering the message from the Druid of the Silures' sacred grove.

"I thank you, Caractacus," said Diviticus, as he embraced them both at once. "I must return him a message with you, as we have much to discuss after our meeting at the Isle of Mona."

Diviticus stood back in appraisal of Caractacus and Venutius. "You have both grown since I saw you last," he said, glancing approvingly at them as he smoothed his long, white robes. "And," he added, "you stroll with the grace of a warrior. You have trained long with the sword and the lance." He paused, beaming with joy seen rarely in a man of such dignified countenance. "You show," he continued, "the promise of a Celtic chieftain."

"And," he said, "I must show you the news of the journey of the stars across the evening sky. We at Mona learned much from Arthnovotus, the Tricerbantes Druid. For many seasons, he has been a student of the skies. And now, he has learned of new stars to guide the traveler upon his journey."

"But," he continued, "we must not talk now. You have come, I know, for a strand of the finest mistletoe which twines about the oak of the sacred grove. I must not keep you from your quest. We shall talk as we meet again to study the stars when the moon rises in the evening sky."

At this, Venutius pulled from his traveling sack the speckled brown trout wrapped in the grasses of the riverbank. "We have brought you a gift from the waters of the Devon," he said, as he thrust the fish into Diviticus' hands.

"What pleasure you have added to my evening meal," he said, as he held the fish between his hands. "It has been long since I have tasted the bounty of the river. We will share our thoughts around the fire of an evening meal when you return," he added.

"We must be off," said Caractacus, "but we shall return as the stars rise in the evening sky."

They turned to wave, sealing their promise of return, as they parted the brush at the edge of the clearing, but Diviticus had disappeared into his hut to prepare the symbols of the evening's sacred rites. Boudicca giggled as she danced along the path in preparation for the maiden's dance. Caractacus and Venutius scanned carefully the mistletoe of every oak, Venutius climbing one to search out the end of its vine, making Boudicca laugh. As he reached the top, he pointed past a stand of maples to a great, ancient oak, partially hidden from view.

"We have found our mistletoe," he shouted, as he scrambled down the trunk, dropping to the forest floor from its great width. "I shall cut it free," he said, as he moved through the stand of maples, pulling his hunting knife from its bronze scabbard studded with amber and the coral of the sea and lashed securely to his waist as he went. He returned to place the mistletoe, its clusters of shiny, green leaves studded with the tiny, yellow flowers of spring, atop her tresses.

"Oh, Venutius, it is beautiful!" she cried, as she danced about, the mistletoe entwined about her locks, the rays of the sun shining down upon them. "Sequanna will be certain to favor me come Beltane."

"You will be the most beautiful of maidens," said Caractacus. "But, now, we must be off to the hunt, and you must carry the mistletoe back to Diviticus to keep its freshness in the waters of the sacred stream."

Boudicca accompanied Caractacus and Venutius to their mounts at the edge of the grove, waving them on long after they became specks upon the distance of the horizon. As they rode, the hunting party assembled in the great forest beyond, accompanied by servants and pack horses, their saddle bags filled to the brim with banquet leftovers, Catrinellia's contribution to help bind the agreements of council in the open air and camaraderie of the hunt.

Mandorix sat tall astride his horse as Votorix pulled his mount alongside the Silures chief. "We shall await Caractacus and Venutius before giving the signal to begin," he said, shading his face with his hand as he looked through the trees to the plains beyond.

Cunobelinus smiled in assent, relaxing his posture astride his mount. "Mandorix looks fine upon his horse," he said, as he glanced over at the boy patiently awaiting the signal to begin. "He will make a fine chieftain someday. But, soon, you must choose a match for Boudicca. Do you have thought on which tribe you shall settle?"

"There are tribes to the south and to the east which will give strength and nobility to the Coritani," said Votorix. "But, though my greatest duty be to the strength of our ancient tribe, I choose also the chieftain," he added, "for I will never make a match to a king who uses ill his queen."

As he spoke, Caractacus and Venutius rode in, slowing their mounts to take their place alongside the party. Votorix nodded as he raised his hand in signal to the horn blower, whose blast upon the long, bronze horn, sculpted with the image of Danu, god of the hunt, sent the waiting party abruptly into the chase of the woodland stag and the wild boar.

When Boudicca was certain the two princes were no longer in her view, she turned to retrace her steps along the path to Diviticus' hut, her strand of mistletoe carefully within her grasp. As she approached the clearing, she heard voices arising from the bank of the sacred stream. She paused to continue her step lightly, avoiding the twigs of the woodland floor, lest she startle the visitors to the stream of the sacred grove.

As she made her way through the brush and onto the grasses of the clearing which held Diviticus' hut, she turned to see a woman, wrapped in a roughly woven tunic of flaxen hue and holding the hand of a boy the size of Mandorix, his trousers worn but sturdy enough to keep the chill from his childish frame.

"Now, drop the wooden image of Sequanna you have carved into the sacred stream," the woman instructed the boy, still holding fast his hand. The boy flung the image, held tight in the grasp of his free hand, upon the sacred stream, the rush of its waters carrying it to the rapids below.

"Now, we must pray to Sequanna," she said, as she let go his hand to step back slightly from the waters of the stream. "Oh,

Sequanna," she implored, "make this boy's leg whole and well. Make it grow like others, so he may do the work of the gods."

The boy moved backward as well, dragging his leg as he went. "Sequanna," he said, "please make my leg strong so I can plow the earth like Father and grow to be a warrior like my brother Anthropus."

Boudicca announced her presence with the snap of a twig underfoot as she moved toward the two along the edge of the sacred stream. She smiled as she spoke. "Sequanna must hear your pleas," she said, directing her words toward the boy. "She favors those who treat well her image."

The woman spoke next. "Ambiatrix grows with a leg that is lame. But, his spirit grows as whole as any other. He follows the plow more slowly than the rest, but the seeds he sows grow as stoutly from the earth."

"We come often to the sacred stream to ask the blessing of Sequanna," she continued. "We come also to gather the herbs of the sacred grove to lay upon Ambiatrix leg as the stars rise in the evening sky, to soothe its stiffness and aid its growth," she added.

As they spoke, Diviticus appeared alongside, worn from the preparations of the altar. "Greetings, Arithra and Ambiatrix," he said, as he addressed the woman and the boy. "You must come in a fortnight to the sacred grove. We shall perform the rites of Epona, and ask the earth goddess' blessing upon Ambiatrix leg. And," he smiled, looking directly at the boy, "we will weave a special bouquet of sacred herbs to hang upon your door to cast away the evil spirits come Sanheim."

Arithra thanked Diviticus, and turned to Ambiatrix. "Come, my son, we must go," she said.

"You must come to the palace to hide and uncover the boar's tooth with my brother Mandorix," said Boudicca, as she turned toward Ambiatrix. "It gives him great pleasure to romp about with one who has passed the same number of seasons as he."

Ambiatrix answered her invitation with a glow upon his face, images of sharing the games and secrets of childhood with a youth of his own years running through his thoughts. Arithra thanked Boudicca and made ready for the two to depart, to finish the chores which awaited them before the sunset, bringing in the tools of the field, leading in the goat from pasture and the young ones from play, and setting out the bread and cheese of the evening meal. Boudicca and Diviticus watched as they walked across the clearing, returning their waves as they departed through the brush.

"Diviticus, are there medicines to make better Ambiatrix leg?" asked Boudicca, as she stooped to gather in her palm the water of the stream to sprinkle upon the waxy, green leaves of her mistletoe strand.

"Our grove and the plains of the Coritani countryside are full of the balm which heals," answered Diviticus. "The leaves of the cinnamon tree to soothe the colic, the unopened buds of the clove tree to rid us of the cough of the winter chill and the dampness of spring, the wild thyme to cure the mange, the mustard seed for the bite of the scorpion, and the powder of the wild crocus to cure the bite of the mad dog or the madness of the plague."

"But," he continued, "for Ambiatrix, there is no cure but the play of youth, the warmth of the crushed mint leaf at evening upon his lame limb, and his prayers to Sequanna and Epona to add strength to his leg as he grows strong and tall."

He paused, taking from her the mistletoe of her hands to lay upon the waters of the stream, a rock to steady its end upon the bank. "You must care well for your strand of mistletoe, Boudicca," he said, as he kneeled along the bank of the stream, carefully placing the strand beneath its waters. "It is the most sacred of symbols of the ancient Celtic rites. It begs favor of Sequanna come Beltane and casts off the evil spirits at Sanheim. And," he added, "its plump, white berries provide food to the birds of winter. But," he continued, as he turned to her, raising himself to stand erect once more, "the taste of its autumnal fruit brings death to the human who craves it."

"Now," he said, as he turned to walk across the grasses of the clearing, "we must talk of omens. You must watch as the white hare of the grove hops about, to tell by its tracks the outcome of a favor or a quest, a bounty or a battle."

Boudicca followed Diviticus toward his hut, as a white hare, nibbling the grasses of the clearing, scampered zigzag toward the safety of its hole behind a woodland rock. "Now," said Diviticus, "if you count the number of changes a hare seeks as it moves along its path, you will know the answer to the question you seek, an odd number favorable, an even number misfortune."

He quieted as he stalked another hare, moving softly from behind, to catch it unawares as it nibbled its leafy meal, lifting it gently and placing it in Boudicca's outstretched hands. "Now," he said, "throw this brown hare over your left shoulder, and observe its retreat. If it runs to the right it is a favorable omen, to the left an unfavorable sign."

Boudicca practiced divining the signs as the hares of the woodland sought the nourishment of the clearing. But, her thoughts were full of Caractacus and Venutius. Would they bring down the woodland stag and corner the wild boar? And, most of all, when would they return?

Diviticus chuckled, as his eyes followed her glance forward to the edge of the grove from whence her companions had departed their mounts in the direction of the hunt. As he pointed to the sun setting in the western sky, he said, "Perhaps one more omen, and we must watch for Caractacus and Venutius to draw near."

She watched intently as he plucked a hare from gently nibbling the broad, leafy grasses, lifting it as he went. "To implore from Andrasta, the goddess of war, a favorable sign of battle, the hare must be tossed to the left and make tracks for the right," he said, as he lifted the large, brown hare to the height of his left shoulder. As he prepared to drop the animal behind him to the ground, Caractacus and Venutius made their way through the brush and onto the clearing, spent from the labor of the hunt, but with the energy of the evening and the laughter of a job well done. Boudicca rushed to greet them, as Diviticus placed the hare down upon the grasses to taste again its leafy meal.

Caractacus pulled from his traveling sack a bounty of banquet leftovers, their packing overseen by Catrinellia to buoy the appetites of council members bound to seal their agreements of council in the camaraderie and open air of the woodland hunt. "We must feast beneath the evening sky," said Caractacus, as he spread their cloth upon the grasses of the clearing. Diviticus prepared the fire to cook the fish Venutius had brought. They shared their bounty, the smooth, white goat cheese of the palace creamery, the thick, crusty, rye bread of its bakery, the joints of wild boar, and the honeyed sweetness of the game birds, as Diviticus pointed toward the sky, singling out the stars with import to the journey of the traveler.

Caractacus, long interested in the secrets of the stars, gazed intently at the sky as he spread a slab of cheese upon a wedge of bread. Venutius, most interested in the division of lands and routes of trade upon the Continent, watched politely as Diviticus pointed to the sky, lifting a joint of wild boar as he listened. Boudicca spoke. "I must pull my mistletoe from the sacred stream," she said, as she licked her fingers from the stickiness of the glaze of the game bird.

"I shall accompany you, Boudicca," said Venutius. "And, you must show me where your arrows carved from the woodland saplings have fallen upon the trees."

As they strolled the paths of the woodland, moonlight streaming down upon them, Boudicca spoke. "Venutius," she asked, looking up at the slender Iberian prince, "what will be your place as Caractacus becomes king of the Silures?"

"I will be a prince consort," he said, pausing for a moment to look beyond the moonlit trees of the woodland. "I should rightfully be king, but for the Romans upon the Continent," he added. "Cunnobelinus has promised my father a match upon the island."

"And, you, Boudicca," he said, as he looked upon her, "shall be a queen. I have heard that even now Votorix casts about for a suitable match to shore up the ancient strength and nobility of the Coritani tribe."

"Yes," she answered, as she strolled slowly beside him, "but, it shall be some seasons before I shall be joined. I have yet to learn the full ways of royal duties."

They continued on, strolling along in silence, Boudicca kicking softly the pebbles beneath her feet as she went. Suddenly, she snagged her sandal upon the root of a large, oak tree, sending her tumbling toward the woodland floor. Venutius reached out, catching her beneath her elbow to break her fall. As he raised her up, their gazes met, their faces partially aglow in the moonlight, stilled by the rush of new feelings rising within them. Venutius broke the silence. "I shall return," he said, letting go her elbow and brushing stray twigs from about her shoulders, tossed down by the careless ramblings of a scampering squirrel above them. "I shall ride for the Coritani gates come Beltane."

Chapter Five

The Coritani palace was abuzz with activity as sundown drew near to signal the start of Beltane. Minstrels polished their silver pipes, etched with woodland creatures and Magda, the goddess of song. Servants pulled from their wardrobes their most glorious costumes of spring to impress the gods and, in some cases, a lover or two. Nobles polished their gaming skills, to throw their opponents off-guard, and pick up a parcel of land or two.

In her dressing room, Catrinellia primped, choosing a finely woven linen tunic of cerulean blue, bordered by threads of gold, a reminder of her once golden locks, now interrupted by streaks of gray. It took three handmaidens at once to dress her tresses, one to hold the hand mirror, one to sweep her tresses atop her head with a boar's bristle brush, and one to fasten them with golden combs decorated with images of the goddess of fertility.

When she put the finishing touches to her costume, she whisked down the hall to Mandorix's chamber to oversee his costume. A tunic of a rich, earthen hue, sturdy trousers to match, sandals turned in calfskin, a sword hilt sporting the image of Danu, god of the hunt, and a grand, new golden belt buckle, recently turned out by the palace artisans to draw his belt of golden links to a close about his tunic.

In her chamber, Boudicca hummed as she swayed back and forth, practicing the rhythm of the maiden's dance. She dropped her linen tunic, woven from the flax of the field to her taste, in the hues of the meadow, the woodland, and the riverbank, over her head as she danced. She secured it with a golden fibula studded with amber and coral at her left shoulder and a brightly hued sash in a woven braid about her waist, adding soft sandals and an armlet of gold. She called Mattillia to dress her tresses, securing the tiny plaits with baubles of amber and coral, the rest wound about with petals of the woodland rose. Atop this creation, she wound her strand of mistletoe. As she dressed, she thought of Venutius.

As she turned to leave, she rubbed her bare arms with rose petals, gathered from the woodland and held fresh in a golden bowl, the robins of the forest chasing each other about its rim. Then, as she walked the hallways, she looked about for Catrinellia and Votorix, to join the procession of revelers streaming through the gates of the Coritani city toward the great hillside beyond. As she searched the hallways, groups of revelers laughing and chatting about her, she saw Mandorix running toward her, his favorite bronze stick for field games tucked securely in the crook of his arm, with Catrinellia not far behind. As he reached her, out of breath from his hallway jaunt, Catrinellia announced her presence.

"Boudicca," she said, as she smoothed a crease of her tunic, "we must hurry to reach the festivities. We must not be late for you to take your place among the maiden's dance." She paused, searching about for Votorix, who was strolling the halls from the far end, lost in talk with a noble in charge of trade. She awaited his presence, and the four joined the procession, strolling through the great stone gates, down the hillside, and out onto the meadow, the stars already in the sky, the tall grasses of the meadow sparkling in the moonlight.

Great bonfires blazed about the hillside as they neared it, with playing fields laid out upon the meadow below. Jugglers practiced their skill in the shadows of the dusk, and minstrels piped their tunes to the birds, now still among the treetops, awaiting the signal to begin. Farmers drove their cattle to be blessed and drive the evil spirits from them. Maidens streamed to the hillside in the vivid hues of springtime to ask the blessings of bounty from Sequanna. And youth, polishing their sporting skills as they went, adorned in their finest trinkets of gold, drawn upon their bodies in the indigo of the leaves of the woad plant, hastened to the hillside to beat their childhood rivals upon the playing fields.

As they reached the hillside, Boudicca spied Linnea standing along the grasses, keeping from the hazards of the bonfires a group of cattle and several small sisters and brothers. Boudicca broke forth from the procession, running toward her friend and throwing her arms about her as she reached her. True to her word, Linnea had managed a coarse linen tunic, woven in the hue of the woodland gorse, her long, golden tresses decked out in the riverbank's daisies.

"Oh, Linnea," said Boudicca, as she embraced her friend, "Sequanna will be certain to bless us." She added, as she stood back, "I have brought the larder's best oat cakes and the freshest woodland rose petals to strew about the feet of her image."

"And, I have brought cakes of rye," said Linnea, giggling at the rush of her friend's words, "and petals of the meadow daisies and the riverbank gorse."

As they stood, Votorix climbed upon a straw hassock to signal the start of the festivities, deferring to Diviticus, who stood upon the hillside in his purest white robe, with a sweep of his arm. As the hush of anticipation swept through the crowd, Votorix raised his arm in signal, and several short blasts of the horn rang out into the stillness of the evening. Minstrels played their pipes, jugglers began to juggle, and youth squared off for the field games of the evening.

Boudicca took leave of Linnea to follow Mandorix to the playing fields of Carabi, where players pummeled silver balls along the grasses with sticks of bronze to a hole at the end of the field, drawing the balls away from the other team. As she went, she saw Ambiatrix dragging his leg after him to stand at the edge of the crowd. Mandorix, she noticed, spied him, too. As players were picked for teams, and given a symbol, Mandorix's name was called.

"I shall play the game upon the field, "he said, the crook of his bronze stick firmly within his grasp, "but I shall need a mate to hit my balls into the field of play and upon the winner's hole." He paused, pointing to Ambiatrix. "I choose him," he said, holding carefully his stick as he spoke, "Let the points we both gain add to the score of our team."

A murmur went up from the crowd, but the gamekeeper, taken with the spirit of the evening, gave his assent. "Let the game begin," he shouted, as he blew upon a special tin pipe three short blasts. At that, both teams descended upon the three silver balls, lined along the middle between them. Mandorix managed to free one, gaining a shot at the winner's hole. Ambiatrix moved to the ball, striking it with the foot of Mandorix's bronze stick, sending it to the edge of the winner's circle, and drawing a gasp from his teammates and a round of cheers from the crowd of onlookers.

As the game progressed, Mandorix's team pummeled many balls toward the target hole, but their opponents, excelling as runners, managed to topple them, drawing in the end the highest score and a congratulatory grasp of the arm. After the tally, Ambiatrix dragged his leg slowly after him to reach Mandorix.

"I have practiced long with a wooden ball my brother Anthropus has carved and the wood of a hickory tree," he said, as he stood in front of Mandorix. "I have sent the ball across the plains when I have come in from the field and the plow. But, I thought only the gods would know the strength I have built in my arms as I swung the stick against the wood of the ball." He paused, shuffling his feet to give comfort to his leg. "I give you my thanks. I shall remember this night as I walk behind the plow of planting time."

Ambiatrix took his leave, the glow of triumph still upon his face, to seat himself upon a rock to watch the evening's festivities. As he sat, Bibrocus, long a minstrel, still spry despite the passing seasons, and filled with the energy of the evening danced up, playing a tune upon his pipe. "May I stop to rest alongside you upon this rock?" he asked, as he stopped his dance to look upon the boy. Ambiatrix nodded assent, glad to get a look so close at pipes which had brought such happy tunes to festivals past.

"I saw your prowess upon the playing field," said Bibrocus, as he seated himself in a nook of the craggy rock. "It takes great courage," he added, "to spend so many seasons long in practice."

"I try to match the courage of my father's father and his father before him," said Ambiatrix. "My father tells us often tales of his great-grandfather, a great warrior in battle against the Romans. And, his grandfather, a warrior who kept the gates of the Coritani free from the invaders of the south. My brothers pass many seasons practicing the skills of the chariot and the sword. I, too, must hold our honor to someday become a warrior as well."

Bibrocus looked long into the distance before he spoke. "There are many ways to hold the honor of the battlefield," he said, as he turned toward Ambiatrix. "Many minstrels have performed with honor upon the field of battle," he said. "My great-grandfather moved with the Silures to chase the Romans under Caesar from our isle." He paused to shift his weight as he spoke. "It is true that it is the warrior who topples the enemy with his sword, but it is the horn blower who in the forefront of battle leads him there. And, often, it is the minstrel, with several loud blasts upon the horn, who frightens the enemy into retreat."

Bibrocus paused, watching Ambiatrix give thought. "Would you like to try my silver pipe?" he asked, passing toward the boy the one with the gods of Beltane etched upon it. Ambiatrix took the ancient and carefully crafted instrument into his hands, a look of awe upon his face. He turned toward Bibrocus. "But, I do not know how to play such an instrument," he said.

"It is easy," said Bibrocus, keeping carefully a smile from breaking out upon his face, as he remembered the first time his father had handed him a silver pipe. "Just blow into the mouthpiece and you will see," he added.

Ambiatrix blew a long, loud sound, with wind from lungs grown strong behind the plow and on the plains of gaming practice. "Well, you see," said Bibrocus, "you already have a natural talent. Now, cover one of those holes and blow, and hear what you shall get."

Ambiatrix covered one of the holes along the pipe with his middle finger, blowing a stronger and higher sound, a look of pleasure mingling with the surprise upon his face. As he lowered the pipe, he noticed his father and brothers driving their herd of cattle toward the path between the two great bonfires set aside for the blessing and purification of livestock. He rose, handing the pipe to Bibrocus. "I must go now," he said, as he shifted his weight to move toward his father's herd. "I must help Father drive the herd to the bonfires of blessing."

Bibrocus rose also, preparing himself to dance among the revelers. "You must come to see me often," he said, as he moved his feet to step lively once again. "We will tap the patience you had to learn the skills of gaming upon the plains to play the tunes of the pipes and of the lyre."

As Ambiatrix moved toward his family's herd of cattle, Boudicca moved toward Diviticus standing on the hillside above them, waiting to bless the livestock. "Diviticus," she asked, gasping slightly from her jaunt up the hill, "when will be the maidens dance?"

"Soon," he said, as the gentle breeze played with the folds of his robes. "When we shall have said the prayers and begged the blessings of bounty from the gods upon all the cattle the Coritani farmers drive between the two great bonfires of blessing. Also," he added, "we must prepare the rites of celebration to honor those who have departed for the Otherworld."

As he said the blessings upon the last of the herds of cattle, he stepped down from his perch above them. Boudicca, anxious for the maidens dance to begin, begged to help with the symbols of the Otherworld rites. "Diviticus," she asked, "why do we celebrate the journey to the Otherworld?"

"Because, Boudicca," he said, as he walked toward the altar he had set up upon the hillside, "it is a happy journey. The Celt that passes to the Otherworld finds a land of plenty, where the richest food and drink flows in abundance, where tree branches sway and birds of bright hued plumes warble songs of beauty from them. Music sounds from pipes and lyres without the touch of a minstrel, spring flowers rise through every season, the pleasures of love are untarnished by guilt, and sickness and decay are banished."

"I will help set up the altar," said Boudicca, as she followed along, lifting her tunic to keep the pace of Diviticus' longer strides. As they reached the altar, Boudicca watched as Diviticus lifted two caged doves, their cooing clear despite the noise of the crowd, from the grassy hillside to place them upon the altar. He directed Boudicca to gather the samples of elaborately prepared food he had carried to the hillside in a large, carefully crafted covered wicker basket to place upon the altar next to a cask of wine. A silver pipe lay aside the two caged doves. And, all about were the newly risen woodland flowers of spring.

"We shall begin," said Diviticus, as a large crowd gathered about the altar along the grasses of the hillside. As he began chanting the ancient rites of the Otherworld, a look of joy upon his face, a hush fell upon the crowd, comfortably cool in the gentle breeze of the evening. When he finished blessing the food, dabbed with honey to show the sweetness of the Otherworld, the flowers, the silver pipe and the wine, he lifted carefully the wooden door of the cage, releasing the doves to fly away swiftly into the night. "Go, and the gods speed you along, our feathered friends," he said, lifting his right arm expansively as he spoke. "Go swiftly," he added, his voice loud and strong in the quiet of the night, "as the spirits of our departed fly to the Otherworld." The crowd, silent until now, waved their arms and cheered, and lifted skins of ale and wine to revel in the rite of celebration.

Diviticus lay his hands upon the altar to end the rite, then turned to Boudicca. "Now, we must begin the maiden's dance," he said, as he stepped down from the altar to walk the grasses of the hillside. Boudicca lifted her tunic, running swiftly down the hillside to the plains below. There, in the meadow, stood a great likeness of Sequanna, sculpted from the oak of the sacred grove, many times the size of the human figure, surrounded by the daisies of the field and lit by the beams of the moon. Maidens, clad in the softest hues of spring, had begun to gather about it. As Boudicca took her place among them, Linnea ran toward her. "Boudicca," she said, as she gasped to catch her breath from her run, "Father has told me he has made a match for me upon the hillside this evening."

"Oh, Linnea," she said, as she embraced her friend, pulling back to pause and ask, "Who shall it be?"

"It is Anthropus," she said, a sigh of relief upon her lips. "But," she added, "it will be many seasons before we shall be joined. Father has driven a hard bargain, and Anthropus must work long and hard to raise a dowry suitable to the agreement he has made with Anthropus' father."

"Oh, Linnea," said Boudicca, as she laughed to share her friend's good fortune, "you shall have such a happy life. And," she added, "you must ask Sequanna's blessings of bounty upon it."

As they spoke, minstrels gathered to pipe the tunes and crowds gathered to witness the maiden's dance. As Boudicca took her place in the circle about Sequanna's great likeness, she spotted Venutius in the gathering crowd, his gaze upon her. She returned his gaze as she lifted her foot to begin the steps of the maiden's dance.

The strains of the minstrels' tunes rose above the murmur of the crowd as maidens, clad in the spectrum of hues, tossed the blossoms of spring, gathered about the Coritani countryside, its meadows, its woodlands, its riverbank, and its plains which stretched as far as its horizon, at the feet of the wooden idol, the scents of the blossoms mingling to rise into the crispness of the evening air. As the music stopped, the maidens moved as one to kneel at the feet of the likeness of the harvest goddess, pressing their offerings of the grain of the Coritani fields, baked into tiny cakes, about the idol's feet. As they knelt, Diviticus prayed from the hillside, to ask for bounty to rise once again from the fields of the Coritani, and to ask the blessings of heirs, a strength to the Coritani, and a legacy to the centuries of traditions of the Celts.

As he finished, the maidens rose, clasping hands as they raised their arms to spread about the idol in a circle once again. Dropping hands, as the minstrels took up their pipes, they began their dance anew, relieved that their prayers had been offered so clearly into the night, with a step more lively and laughter all around. The crowd cheered, and the families of the dancers rushed forward, embracing the dancers as they went.

Catrinellia was first to reach Boudicca. She embraced her daughter, standing back, her hands remaining still upon her shoulders. "Boudicca," she said, as she looked full upon her face, "you are now a Celtic maiden. We must work hard to make you worthy of that privilege." As she backed away, Votorix rushed forward, choking with emotion as he wrapped Boudicca in his

70

embrace. "Boudicca," he said, slowly letting go his arms about her, "you have made me very proud. I wish always the blessings of the gods upon you."

Mandorix came forward as well, offering an embrace and a request to once again rejoin the games. Catrinellia gave him her permission, as she and Votorix prepared to circulate once again among the crowd. Boudicca rushed over to Linnea, squeezing her hands within her own, their giggles rising above the nearby laughter. As Linnea rejoined the festivities, a gaggle of brothers and sisters hanging about her, Boudicca searched the crowd to spy Venutius. As she stood, she felt a hand upon her shoulder. She turned to look directly into Venutius' face.

"Oh, Venutius," she said, as she threw her arms about him, "you have come as you have promised. We must take a walk to celebrate," she laughed, as she let go her embrace.

They walked past the knots of celebrants as they strolled across the meadow. "You must tell me all the news of Caractacus and your journey on the mission of trade," said Boudicca, looking up at Venutius as they strolled through the tall grasses of the meadow, clumps of buttercups and bluebells risen with the spring rains among them.

"Caractacus is longer in council and less upon the plains or at the woodland hunt," said Venutius, as he strolled slowly beside her. "Cunobelinus is tired, and wishes soon to pass on the mantle of chieftain. Caractacus studies carefully, for he fears Roman unrest upon the Continent, and he must learn as well the tactics to keep the strength of the Silures from the fierce tribes of the south which attack the gates and raid the fields."

"Cunobelinus has assigned to me the order of the nobles' lands," said Venutius, as he continued to stroll beside her, "and, in respect for my father, whose ancestors, before the Roman conquest, were tribal chieftains, he has assigned to me to open further the routes of trade upon the Continent."

"Caractacus is pleased with this assignment," he added, "as he has bade me to listen as I travel to talk of the Roman empire, to allow him warning to make alignments if Rome makes plans to sail in ships of conquest for our shores."

Venutius finished his talk as they reached the edge of the sacred grove. "Oh, Venutius," said Boudicca, "we must walk through the grove to ask the blessings of Beltane from Sequanna along the sacred stream where she lies most pure."

Venutius chuckled as he parted the brush for the pair to reach the open path. As they trod the path, Venutius reached for the limb of an ancient oak. "I shall carve you a likeness of Sequanna that you may fling upon the waters of the stream and secure her fullest blessings," he laughed, as he pulled from the sheaf about his waist a short hunting knife to part from the limb a hefty branch.

They trod the paths to reach the stream and dropped upon the grasses beside its waters. Venutius whittled slowly in the moonlight, the branch of the oak soon a likeness of the Beltane goddess. He stood, and lifted Boudicca to her feet as he handed her gently the likeness of Sequanna. As she flung the oaken likeness upon the waters, Venutius put his hands upon her shoulders to turn her toward him. "Boudicca," he said, as he looked down upon her, "I leave soon for the Continent. But, I shall send you word as I go."

He bent down to kiss her upon her lips, the scent of the blossoms entwined in her tresses wafting about them. As he pulled back, he took her hands in his. "I shall return," he said, as he looked upon her face aglow in the moonlight, "and when I do, we will ride the plains and pick the blossoms along the banks of the Devon River and tread the woodland paths of the sacred grove as we always have."

They walked back across the meadow, lost in small talk and in silence, the future crowding their thoughts. They reached the hillside as the Beltane announcements had just begun, births and justice meted out, new landowners, new marriage banns, and those who had gone through the rites of Beltane passage. As Diviticus was handing down these pronouncements, then Votorix took his place upon the hassock above the crowd, silencing it by his presence.

"I would like to make an announcement," he said, as only the noise of crickets rose to fill the silence. He paused, then continued. "I have made a match for the Princess Boudicca. She will be joined with the King Prasutagus, chieftain of the mighty Iceni tribe. May the match be bountiful, and our two tribes prosper together."

As he spoke, Boudicca and Venutius stood, silently clasping hands at the edge of the crowd.

Chapter Six

Servants scurried about the Iceni palace halls, tossing blossoms of violets, daisies, and larkspur, plucked from the carefully cultivated gardens of the palace atrium. The palace bakers turned out great loaves of bread, heavy with rye, and tiny, honeyed oat cakes. Grooms brushed ceremonial mounts in the palace stables, and fed them stores of special oats. And servants, drawn from everywhere, dug pits upon the hillside, to turn the great stores of game, brought down in the vast forests of Iceni lands, enough for a seven day feast, over an open fire.

In the largest guest chamber of the Iceni palace, Boudicca peered into a looking glass a handmaiden held to inspect her costume for the gala ceremony that would unite her with Prasutagus and make her queen of the Iceni tribe. Handmaidens hovered about her, ready to attend to her every whim. Urns of the most delicate and pungent scents, pressed from the finest oils of the Continent, surrounded her. Bowls of petals dried from the violet, the hyacinth, and the hawthorn blossom lined the shelf above her.

Throngs had gathered already along the meadow and upon the hillsides below the Iceni city, from the island's distant and neighboring tribes, from the Iceni cities, and from the Iceni countryside. Boudicca gazed into the looking glass, pinching her cheeks to bring them color, and smoothing the lines about her eyes and mouth. She must be radiant, for much was riding on this match.

As she arranged the folds of her tunic, she thought of Venutius and Caractacus. In the five Beltanes which had passed since Votorix had announced her match upon the Coritani hillside, Caractacus had become king of the Silures in a ceremony which she had attended, and had soon made Cortitiana his queen. Venutius had opened trade routes which still thrived upon the Continent, and had been called home to oversee the Silures lands. He had visited her often after the announcement of her match, but he had honored the promise of its troth, strolling about the meadows and the woodlands, chatting with Diviticus, and roaming the sacred grove.

Her tunic hung about her, a finely woven linen spun from the flax of the Coritani fields, turned the purest white, the edges embroidered with bands of sacred white geese. She gathered the waist with a belt of golden squares, its buckle a likeness of the goddess Danu, a gift from Prasutagus, and fastened its shoulder with a silver fibula, its clasp imbedded with tiny chunks of amber. White leather sandals with long, soft ties were laced about her ankles. She added a golden armlet which twisted about her arm in a likeness of the goddess Magda, and a heavy golden torque, its clasp twin likenesses of the earth goddess Epona's horses. She added as well an anklet of fine, gold chain, a gift of childhood, and a coral ring, large and simply cut, from Prasutagus' dowry.

She called for Mattilia to dress her tresses as she sat upon the bench of the large, oaken dressing table of the chamber, its legs each turned with pairs of tiny songbirds. Although clusters of Iceni handmaidens stood about, it was Mattilia, her locks now slightly grayed but her gait still sprightly, who knew how to coax the long, thick locks to bend to brush and comb. Mattilia made her way through the knots of handmaidens to the dressing table, lifting from the shelf above it the brush with the stiffest of boar's bristles and the thickest of amber handles. She brushed Boudicca's tresses atop her head, fastening some with tiny combs of gold, catching others with the blossoms of the Iceni palace gardens, and winding some about in tiny braids fastened with beads of coral. The rest she left to hang about in tiny wisps and curls.

Boudicca rose, splashing scents from the tiny urns upon her bare arms, mingling the spicier scents of the Far East with the sweeter scents of the Continent. Then, she walked through the doorway of the chamber and down the Iceni palace hallways, sculpted battle scenes, woodland hunts, and festival rites lining their walls. Handmaidens followed, strewing rose petals all about her. She walked through the great, double oak doors of the palace, and through the heavy, timber gates which led to the Iceni city, and down the grasses of the hillside, shorn low for the ceremony, to the meadow below.

Her mount waited at the foot of the hillside, a large, white stallion, a gift of Votorix to fill the loss of Tricerbantes' passing. She had named him Palingetorix, a name she had given to a riverbank tortoise she once had kept as a pet. Carefully groomed and saddled, he pawed the ground, waiting for a touch of the reins to guide him. With the aid of the head stable servant, she climbed upon the mount, nudging him slowly forward. Handmaidens clustered about her, arranging the folds of her tunic.

As her mount moved forward, she searched the crowd for Venutius. He had promised to be with her on this day, sending word by messenger, and assuring her of his presence with every visit. She knew Caractacus would not be at his side. He had sent word of raiders upon the Silures fields, keeping him busy upon the field of battle, and Cortitiana was soon to bear a royal heir. As she searched the throngs, many already heady with flasks of wine and ale, she spied Venutius standing along her path, clad in the sturdy leather trousers of the hide of the woodland stag, a tunic of crimson hue edged in gold, the Silures emblem upon it, and a ceremonial bronze sword about his waist, its scabbard hilt a likeness of Sylvanius, god of the hunt. Their gazes met as she passed.

Tribal chieftains lined the meadow, vying with nobles and merchants, artisans and farmers for a glimpse of the royal rites. As she moved along, Boudicca spied Cartimandua, now queen of the great Brigantes tribe, her black locks piled elaborately atop her head, her tunic woven from threads of gold, the heavy torque about her neck a likeness of the goddess of battle, Andrasta. Handmaidens hovered about her. As Boudicca passed, though Cartimandua kept her eyes upon the procession and the features of her carefully composed face unmoved, their gazes did not meet.

Farther along, Boudicca spied Linnea, clad in a coarse, linen tunic, its hue the blended greens of the Coritani countryside. Her tinkling laughter rose above the crowd. Spared from the labor of the fields and duties of the family, she was here to honor a pact they had made long ago as giggling youth running about the banks of the Devon River, to share their fortunes.

Ahead at the edge of the meadow, Prasutagus waited astride a great roan mount, decked out with a saddle cloth of the brightest hues and a ceremonial bridle bit of bronze. His tunic was the deepest blue of the woad plant, its edges embroidered in gold, the Iceni crest upon it. A thick, gold, twisted torque hung about his neck and a large, bronze, ceremonial sword about his waist. His pale, blue eyes were steady, and his long, blond locks and beard, carefully trimmed for the ceremony, though he was nearly twenty years her senior, remarkably free of grey.

Votorix stood nearby, flanked by Catrinellia and Mandorix upon the grasses of the meadow, pride upon his face. Not far stood Astrinellia, the only sister of Prasutagus, a slight limp the result of a childhood illness, clad in a simple, linen tunic of violet hue. Boudicca guided her mount alongside Prasutagus and signaled him to stop. A host of Iceni Druids stood upon the hillside, Diviticus among them, with all manner of symbols of the gala rite.

The chief Druid signaled to begin, and the crowd hushed, straining to hear the chanting of the rites. The Druids, clad in their finest ceremonial robes, shouted pleas to every Celtic god and showered offerings upon them. The Iceni gods, held special to the tribe, were revered with special offerings.

Diviticus chanted a prayer for a long and happy union filled with the greatest bounty. He raised his hands as he spoke. "May the queen of the Iceni prosper, and may this union bring strength and great bounty to our tribes."

The Iceni Druids chanted again in unison, lifting the symbols of the rite as they spoke. the wheat of the Iceni fields, the doves of harmony and peace, the blossoms of the Iceni woodlands and of its gardens, and a boar's foot, symbol of the bounty of the hunt.

Then, they came down from the hillside, forming a circle about the royal couple, bidding them to join hands as symbol of the union. Boudicca and Prasutagus reached across the tall grasses of the meadow to clasp hands. The Druids intoned one last prayer, an ending to the rite.

The crowd cheered, tossing blossoms of meadow daisies, bluebells and larkspur they had plucked, or passing round the skins of wine and ale. Boudicca and Prasutagus rode off to the edge of the great woodland which ran beside the meadow, a signal for the festivities to begin. As they dismounted their horses, well-wishers surrounded them. Nobles to curry favor with the new political alignment, the curious, merchants and farmers alike, from the reaches of the Iceni borders, and guests from the tribes of the island.

Boudicca stood in front of a great oak tree as Votorix came toward her, taking great strides across the meadow. Catrinellia and Mandorix followed. Votorix wrapped his great arms around her. "I know you will carry well the mantle that has been thrust upon you, Boudicca," he said, as he loosened his embrace to look upon her. "I know you will bring the joys of the Coritani and perform well the duties you have studied faithfully for so long. May peace be with you always, my daughter."

Catrinellia approached Boudicca, silent as she embraced her. She stood back as she spoke. "I will pray for you, Boudicca," she said, her long, red tunic flowing about her. "May you perform well your duties."

Mandorix then stepped forward, uncertain to embrace her, his frame newly grown tall and gangling, his once blond locks nearly white grown darker and longer about his shoulders. "I shall visit you often," he said, as his arms hung about his sides. "I shall still come for stories of Sandheim."

Boudicca laughed, as she stepped forward to embrace him. "I shall think up new stories as I ride the woodland paths and stroll about the meadows. And, you must bring Ambiatrix with you," she added. "I would so like him to see the great Iceni playing fields and strike a ball upon them."

Mandorix turned to follow Votorix and Catrinellia to join the festivities, already beginning across the meadow's grasses. As he went, Cartimandua replaced him to stand before her, followed by an entourage of servants. She stared directly into Boudicca's eyes, her eyes unmoving as she spoke. "Prasutagus has long ruled wisely the Iceni tribe," she said, pausing after she spoke. She continued. "I hope you will be an asset to him." At that, she turned abruptly, to return to the festivities, followed again by the host of servants.

As she stood, Boudicca spied Linnea hanging about the edge of the crowd, awaiting a turn to greet her. Linnea came forward, throwing her arms about her. "Oh, Boudicca," she said, as she stood back to admire Boudicca's costume. "You look so grand," she said. "I shall hardly know how to describe your tunic to Anthropus," she added. She took a deep breath to slow the words which had come tumbling so rapidly out. "I must remember your costume, the ceremony, and the celebration. Mama made me promise. And," she added, stopping again to take a breath, "I must remember for the little ones."

Boudicca smiled. "I shall give you a memento of the ceremony," she said, as she reached for the saddlebag upon her mount. She pulled from it a small, coral ring, part of her ceremonial offering to the gods, and pressed it into Linnea's palm.

"Oh, Boudicca," she said, wordless as her hands closed about it, "I shall treasure it always." She paused. "It will help me to remember," she added, "as I plow the fields or gather the little ones in from the countryside as the sun sets upon the meadows the seasons we spent along the banks of the Devon."

"You must visit when you can," said Boudicca. "We shall find a stream or woodland path to walk along. I must hear of Anthropus, and how plentiful are the fish and the frogs of the Devon River."

"Anthropus has promised," answered Linnea. "He has promised to spare me in the season after we reap the harvest of our fields." She paused. "I must go now," she said, as she stood back. "Papa will miss my mount upon the fields." They embraced once again, and Linnea turned to stride across the meadow to the small grove of newly flowered hawthorn trees where her mount was safely lashed.

Boudicca turned to stroll among the crowd, by now feasting upon the succulence of the boar turned upon the spit and the tiny game birds roasted over an open pit, swapping stories of political rebuffs and maneuvers of every kind, of gossip of the palace and the marketplace, passing round skins of wine and ale, and gaming for stakes remembered barely in the morning on game boards of silver and gold.

As Boudicca passed among them, Astrinellia stood beneath a great oak tree, the sun's rays barely shining through its widespread branches, the violet of her tunic a blend with the mossy floor and leafy green of the woodland. She stepped forward to greet Boudicca, her lameness barely visible as she went.

"Boudicca," she said, as she greeted her with an embrace, "I shall be a sister to you always." She stepped back, her leg dragging only slightly. Her face wan, her pale, blue eyes reflected the hue of her violet tunic, and her long, blond locks were caught up in a single, violet bow.

"I have long been my brother's keeper," she said, as she shifted her weight as she spoke. "I have looked after his affairs as he went upon the field of battle, or sat in council, or talked to merchants of trade, or rode about the countryside in search of answers to the affairs of state."

"When Father was chieftain of this tribe, there was no match for me upon this island," she continued. "And, a match within the nobility of this tribe would have weakened the royal family." She paused. "Since that time," she added, "I have been devoted to the Iceni palace, its kitchens and its larder, its spinning rooms, its chambers, and its atrium gardens, and to Prasutagus, smoothing the way for tribal guests, the meetings of Druid justice, and councils of tribal affairs upon our island."

"Now that you are queen, I shall step aside" she said, shifting her weight upon the woodland floor. "But," she added, "I shall be always at the ready to give the aid or advice you need as you will it."

Boudicca embraced Astrinellia. As she stood back, she spoke. "We shall work together, Astrinellia," she answered. "I have much to learn of Iceni ways." She paused. "I shall never try to replace you in Prasutagus' mind or heart."

Astrinellia reached for Boudicca's hand, taking it into hers. "I welcome you into the Iceni tribe," she said. "May your bounty be great."

As Astrinellia took her leave to move among the guests, Boudicca spied Venutius, standing beneath a sycamore, his gaze upon her. She moved toward him, lifting her tunic slightly as she went. As she came upon him, she lifted her face toward his and spoke. "Venutius," she said, "we must take one last stroll together."

"Boudicca," he answered, as he turned to join her to tread the woodland paths, "I promise this shall not be our last stroll. I shall visit as often as the routes of trade and nobles' squabbles let me." They strolled, in silence, violets and anemones newly sprung along the mossy woodland paths, shaded by sycamores, oaks, and hawthorns. As they reached a stream in the forest, Venutius reached to bend a sycamore branch, green and supple in its youth, pulling a short, hunting knife from its sheath about his waist to cut it swiftly down.

He began to carve, a smile upon his face. "I shall again carve for you a likeness of Sequanna," he said, chuckling as he chipped away shavings of the sycamore branch. "We shall ask again the bounty of the river goddess."

Boudicca stood at the edge of the stream gazing upon its fast-flowing waters rushing headlong to the rapids below, the rays of the sun bouncing off her tresses. As Venutius finished his carving, he handed her the likeness of the goddess. "Now you must cast it upon the waters once again," he said, as he stepped nearer to her at the edge of the stream. Boudicca flung the tiny idol onto the rapidly flowing waters, following it along with Venutius its path with their gazes as it went.

Venutius spoke. "We must return to the festivities, Boudicca" he said, as he stepped back from the edge of the stream. He paused. "I ride for the Silures palace on the morrow. But, I promise, I shall send word often of visits and bring news of our tribe, the tribes upon our isle and the Continent." They arrived back at the edge of the forest, wordless as they strolled, and parted.

As the sun set, servants built great bonfires, games were played upon the hillside, and the feasting continued, depleting the palace larder by the hundreds of boar, game birds, and woodland stag. When the stars had been long risen in the sky, Prasutagus moved about to search for Boudicca, finding her urging on the board game of two young nobles. Cheers and guffaws rose from the crowd, the stakes of the game nearly lost among the noise, the golden pieces poised in standoff along the silver board, the players hunched forward in tense anticipation. Prasutagus hesitated slightly, then reached out his hand to clasp Boudicca's, drawing her toward him. As she reached him, he let go her hand, and spoke. "Boudicca," he said, "we must return to the palace, as on the morrow we shall be expected to lead the festivities once again." He led her across the meadow as he spoke, graciously fending off the well-wishers who were still coming upon him as he went.

They walked up the hillside below the city and through its gates thick with boulders and oaken beams, and toward the palace entrance, its great oak doors flung back. They entered the great halls of the palace, decked everywhere with blooms of field, woodland, and atrium gardens. The scent of blossoms rose about them, as they strolled through the winding hallways of the palace toward the royal bedchamber.

Prasutagus led the way, striding slowly, his tall, slender frame lending dignity to his gait. A manservant attended him as he went. Boudicca followed, a bevy of handmaidens at her side, laughing and chattering as they went, the excitement of the evening's festivities hovering over them still.

They reached the bedchamber and entered it, Prasutagus clearing its entrance only slightly. Its great clay floors held oaken chests and urns of every kind. Its bed a mass of the softest skins, its bedcovers, plentiful and thick, an indigo hue, and its silken drapes the hues of sunrise. The stars shone through windows all about, their shutters still flung open.

An adjoining chamber held a large, oaken dressing table and chests for garments of every kind. "Boudicca," said Prasutagus, "you shall prepare in yonder chamber. Veronnia," he added, motioning toward the handmaiden in charge, "will aid you. The chamber chests are filled with garments fashioned especially to suit you."

Boudicca walked toward the chamber accompanied by Veronnia. As she entered, she spied chests of every woodland tree lining the walls. She lifted their lids. In one, neatly folded tunics of finely woven linen in every hue were piled high. In another, woolens in the darker hues of autumn were stacked one upon the other. In another, mantles and cloaks, and in another, sturdy riding trousers, crafted in the toughest hides. In another, a small, cherry wood chest, crafted with the fruits and flowers of the woodland, lay bedclothes of every hue, the deep indigo, the soft greens of the meadow grasses, and the violets, oranges, yellows and blues of the blossoms of woodland and meadow.

Boudicca pulled from the pile a finely woven linen in indigo hue, its tiny flowers and woodland geese embroidered in saffron yellow. Veronnia unclasped the silver fibula which held Boudicca's tunic and draped the indigo linen about her. Boudicca turned toward the great urns which held the water and splashed droplets upon her face, drawn from the excitement of the day, and rubbed some upon her hands, drying them carefully upon a linen cloth Veronnia held. Then, she rubbed handfuls of dry rose petals, held in a small, silver bowl forged with the goddesses of the woodland which sat atop the great, oaken dressing table, upon her bare arms, and splashed woodland scents, held in tiny urns, upon her tresses, let down and brushed by Veronnia.

She rose, dismissed Veronnia and the rest of the handmaidens, and walked into the bedchamber where Prasutagus stood, in nightclothes of saffron yellow. He took Boudicca's hand and led her to the bed, massive with the softest skins framed in timbers of sturdy oak. "Boudicca," he said, as he let go her hand, "I have had many women. My pleasure has never been denied. But," he added, as he looked upon her, "I shall not press you."

"Prasutagus," she answered, looking also upon him, "I am aware of my duty. I am aware also of what this union means to both our tribes. I know that our union is a symbol of it. I shall never deny you."

He took again her hand and climbed upon the bed, drawing her up beside him. As they consummated their union, the evening breeze wafted through the chamber, and the stars shone brightly in the sky through the great, long windows, their shutters still flung back.

Chapter Seven

The snow lay thick upon the ground outside the royal bedchamber as Boudicca gave birth to the first Iceni heir in many seasons. The child's cries rang out, filling the chamber with noisy squalls. Boudicca laughed as she heard the protests of her newborn infant.

Servants attended her, versed in the art of birth, mopping her brow with cool, linen cloth, wrung with the waters of nearby countryside springs, and caring for the afterbirth. The child, a baby girl, continued to shriek, piercing the air with the demanding cries of the newborn. Nursemaids cooed about her and clucked, rocking her gently and sponging her off with a soft, wet linen cloth, wrapping about her as she dried a heavy, woolen wrapper of many hues. They laid the infant at Boudicca's side.

Boudicca pulled the child to her breast, quieting her as she softly stroked her cheek. As the infant suckled, Boudicca took stock of her newborn daughter. A tuft of locks as golden as Prasutagus' once had been. Her face, though red and wizened from birth, held eyes as blue as the robin's egg waiting to be fledged in spring along the riverbank. Her sturdy body lay still as she suckled, and her tiny hands grasped Boudicca's breast, her nails as yet uncut scratching slightly the softness of her skin.

Boudicca beamed down upon her newborn daughter. She would ride the plains and explore the woodlands with her, and teach her to send an arrow she carved from a sapling toward the trunk of a great, oak tree, as she had learned. And, she would take her to visit Diviticus, for he must teach her the ways of the omens of the Celtic gods.

Her name would be Alaina, a name she had chosen and Prasutagus had agreed upon. Chosen from Prasutagus' ancestry, the name had been given to his great-grandmother, a woman of Gallic heritage, a chieftain's daughter, brought to the island as wife to the Iceni king. When her husband had been killed upon the field of battle, she ruled the tribe with wisdom until her eldest son was old enough to become the chief. Large in size, and popular with tribespeople as far as the borders of the tribal lands, her words of wisdom could still be heard repeated among the people of the Iceni tribe.

As Alaina's eyes began to close and her suckling to drop off, Boudicca called for a nursemaid to carry the infant to her nearby cradle. Carved from the great oak of the Iceni woodland, it rested upon a sturdy rocker, its head and footboards turned with tiny songbirds and masses of woodland flowers.

Prasutagus had agreed that Alaina would slumber nearby, so that Boudicca could hear her tiniest cries, to soothe her quickly with a feeding. Boudicca had agreed as well to the occasional feedings of a young servant who had just given birth herself, brought to the royal quarters for the task. But, Boudicca had made it clear that it would be she who would attend as often as she could to her newborn daughter.

Alaina's birth would be cause for rejoicing among the Iceni tribe, for there had been no royal birth for many seasons. Boudicca smiled as she thought of the celebrations to come and how happy the birth would make the Iceni people. Bells would ring, the palace bards would recite new rhymes, and people would feast on ale and tiny, honeyed cakes. The Iceni Druids would prepare a special rite come Beltane in honor of the birth.

As the nursemaid gently lifted Alaina from her bed, Boudicca drifted off to sleep. She knew she must soon regain her strength.

As Boudicca grew stronger, and Alaina older, Boudicca packed the infant into a sack and wrapped her in layers of woolens, leaving free her darting eyes and tiny, turned-up nose. Then, they trod the meadows and the woodlands on horseback, Alaina securely fastened to the saddle of the mount, or wrapped securely in her mother's arms. The two looked about the countryside, still winter, for signs of life.

Dew drops sparkled along the meadow grasses, the morning thick with fog. As it lifted, the two would look for birds, spying a linnet upon a thistle-seed, or a blackbird or thrush singing its morning song. Or, a robin or a sparrow, searching out a perch in a landscape gone to rest.

As they spied a bird, Alaina's piercing, blue eyes would dart toward the creature, and sometimes she would coo. Boudicca would laugh, and explain to her the kind of bird it was, and what was its morning mission. Its song sounded shrill in the morning air.

Birds vied for the red berries of the holly plant and the white berries of the mistletoe which twined around the bark of the apple tree and the oak. Sacred to the Celts, fatal to the human taste, the mistletoe twined about the tree as parasite to feed the birds.

Boudicca sang as they rode, and Alaina often fell asleep. Sometimes, with a few nursemaids to accompany them, they would walk the paths of the woodlands, and spy a hare behind a rock, or a fox, his coat turned grey in the winter, turning to trot across a nearby meadow.

Astrinellia, fond of Alaina, would watch the child also. Although she rarely left the palace, Astrinellia often asked to see the child through to slumber. As nursemaids bathed Alaina and wrapped her in her nightclothes, and scented her with petals dried from woodland flowers, Astrinellia stood by, to gently rock her cradle and sing her to slumber with a lullaby learned long ago from a palace nursemaid.

Tribal affairs filled Prasutagus' days as well as evenings. He came late to the royal bedchamber, long after the stars had risen in the sky, weary from council meetings and the haggling of nobles over lands. He held council with merchants as well on the routes of trade most favorable to Iceni goods. The tin and gold pulled from prolific mines, the bronze turned into sheaths and swords, bridles and bits, enameled and coral studded. Hides of the great Iceni forests turned to sandals and riding trousers. Ploughs and reapers, bowls of silver and gold, gilded and engraved, and silver game boards with playing pieces of gold. All turned by artisans busy at forges and wheels in the daily activity of the Iceni hilltop cities. As Prasutagus lay down upon the great bed, his tall and slender frame weary from the day, Boudicca tried to talk of tribal worries and affairs, but he most often drifted quickly off to slumber.

Boudicca served Prasutagus well in council, making certain that he took his evening meal, a refreshment he often forgot. She coaxed the kitchen servants to pull the most inviting portions from the roasted boars and quail, stag and woodland hares, and tiny game birds brought down in the great Iceni forests. She brought always his meal herself, setting it down beside him upon a small, wooden table, carved with the vines of the woodland. She mingled often with the tradesmen, nobles and warriors in council, charming them with her youth and wit.

Prasutagus often journeyed about the countryside to oversee its progress. Boudicca spent the long evenings when he was gone playing with Alaina, or in conversation or a board game with Astrinellia, or watching the sun set while Astrinellia embroidered upon a cloth of linen.

On the days when Prasutagus was about the palace, as Boudicca became more familiar with Iceni ways, she learned when best to approach him and engage him in the art of conversation. On an evening when the foreboding chill of winter was in the autumn air, Boudicca brought to Prasutagus his evening meal, arranged upon a golden tray. She brought as well a many-hued lap robe to stay the chill of the great hall, its high ceilings and expansive floors of clay chilled despite the efforts of servants to keep them warm with fires banked about them.

"Prasutagus," she began, as she lay the brightly-hued woolen about him, "you are worn with tribal affairs. Perhaps on a morn you could ride the countryside in pleasure or bring down a wild boar in a woodland hunt. Or, challenge a noble to a board game. Perhaps Armandes, for he is the only noble with wit to challenge you upon the gaming table."

"Boudicca," he answered, as he looked up, the lines upon his weary face grown longer, the flecks of gray in his locks and beard grown wider, "it has been long since I have challenged a noble to

91

a board game or risen before the sun to ride about the countryside in search of woodland game."

"But," he continued, "the nobles clamor for attention over lands and merchants squabble over trade. The bars and ingots of one tribe, or the demand of goods for goods of another, do not match the system of Iceni coins. And," he added, shifting his lean weight upon his hassock, "I must often hold council with the artisans of the coin, for the same symbol must be engraved upon each coin, a task resisted by the Celtic craftsman."

Prasutagus paused to lift a joint of roasted wild boar from the golden tray. He continued. "I must also hold council with warriors and nobles. News has come from the Continent that Claudius takes Tiberius' place in Rome as emperor. It is said that he needs a victory to assure his power with the Roman people. He will be certain to attempt what Caesar failed to accomplish upon our isle. There are rumors that he is already planning to send the Roman army across the sea in great number to attack our British tribes, to subdue them as the Iberians and the Gauls."

"What shall we do, Prasutagus?" asked Boudicca.

"I must hold council with the warriors and nobles, before we reach a decision," he answered. "But, I believe if the numbers of the Roman army overwhelm us, or if their strategy surpasses ours, we must lay down our weapons in cooperation. For, if we please the emperor, he might be lenient, allowing us to still bear arms and turn out goods and coins in trade."

"Now," he continued, as he paused to taste the joint of wild boar, "I must prepare to hold council with our merchants. They arrive this evening from towns far toward Iceni borders. They clamor for more trade upon the Continent, for our tin pulls a high exchange, and the work of our artisans sought after, both by the

Celts and by the Roman governors. Our bridle-bits of bronze and woolens, our brightly-hued enameled clasps and buttons are highly prized, and our sandals of sturdy hides."

Boudicca smoothed again the woolen about Prasutagus' shoulders, and turned to make her way across the clay of the great hall's floor. Her woolen tunic, the hues of the spring meadow grasses, hung about her ankles, drawn at her waist by a belt of golden squares, her sandals a softened hide. Her tresses were drawn back in a mass of curls, loosely clasped with tiny, coral beads.

As she swept across the clay floor and out the entrance of the great hall, she turned toward Alaina's chamber. She must feed her daughter and sing her to slumber with a lullaby. She must also attend to the infant's morning costume, she thought, as she strolled more quickly toward the child's chamber. She would lay it out and choose the brightest hue, perhaps the indigo with the tiny woodland flowers embroidered round its edges, for she had had word of a visit from Linnea. She would arrive at Iceni gates on the morrow.

Boudicca arose before the sun to await Linnea's arrival. Linnea rode through the Iceni gates as the sun shone upon her tresses, the morning rays glistening upon her golden locks, loosely hanging round about her shoulders. Her homespun tunic was neatly gathered with a flaxen belt, and her saddlebag was full of gifts gathered about the Coritani countryside. A rock grown smooth from the rush of the Devon's waters. A woodland root, its gnarled tentacles twisted nearly in the shape of a bird of prey. A brightly-hued stone gathered from the river's edge.

Linnea rode through the city gates toward the palace stables. As she dismounted at the entrance, she handed the lead of her mount to a waiting stable servant and ran across the grasses of the courtyard toward the palace entrance, the rough hide of her sandals parting the grasses as she went. Boudicca, strolling about in wait, spied her friend and ran quickly under the timbers of the palace entrance, its oaken doors flung back, across the courtyard to throw her arms about her, bringing a rise of Linnea's hearty laughter.

As Boudicca let go her embrace about Linnea, she stood back to look upon her. Her cheeks were as ruddy as the fruit they had often pulled from the apple trees in an autumn stroll along the woodland paths, and her face aglow as the new rays of the early morning sun.

"You thrive well," said Boudicca, as she led her friend toward the palace entrance. "The long days about the Coritani countryside must be still agreeable."

"This season past, I spent little time about the countryside," answered Linnea, as she followed Boudicca through the palace entrance and along its hallways. "Since Anthropus and I were joined, we have spent long days upon the fields, bringing grain from the earth to store. We help Father, for there are many mouths to feed. And," she added, as she slowed her strides to match Boudicca's, "we pray also to Sequanna for little ones to join us."

"Sequanna shall answer your prayers," laughed Boudicca, looking upon her friend. "We shall pray to her as we cross the Iceni countryside," she said. "But, first," she added, "you must see Alaina."

They walked toward the child's chamber, passing through its heavy, timbered entrance as they reached it. Alaina lay awake in her cradle, cooing with pleasure at the sight of her tiny toes.

Linnea let out a squeal of joy, and begged to carry the infant about the floors of the chamber. Boudicca laughed and lifted the child from her cradle, handing Alaina to her.

Linnea dashed about, laughing and cooing, playing games and reciting the rhymes of childhood. She carried Alaina to the open window, bathing her in the rays of the mid-morning sun. "We shall head for the Iceni countryside," said Boudicca, as she took Alaina to hand her to a waiting nursemaid, giving word to wrap her against the autumn chill.

When Alaina was bundled in several woolen wraps, the three headed for the countryside, on chestnut mares with saddlebags filled with a mid-day meal. They trotted across the meadow, its scarlet poppies swaying in the breeze, their mounts slowed to suit Alaina, though the child often screamed with delight at a short but dashing gallop across the plains.

"We must find a stream and pray to Sequanna," said Boudicca, as they entered the great forest at the meadow's edge. As they entered its woodland, they spied a stream, its banks overflowing, its stones turned smooth from the centuries of its rushing waters, shaded by an old, oak tree. They dismounted, and spread a great woolen cloth of many hues upon its long and aged roots, a clump of snowdrops nestled in its shade, the white of its blossoms a burst of hue against the barren scape of woodland, laying Alaina, still swathed in her woolen wraps, upon it.

Boudicca sat upon the cloth, pulling from her saddlebag their midday meal. A hearty rye turned out in the palace bakery, cheeses of every kind aged in the palace creamery, and tiny, honeyed game birds, chilled in the evening, autumn air. "We shall pray to Sequanna," she said, as she turned to share the fare with Linnea. Linnea rose and tossed the petals of a nearby woodland rose, the last of autumn, upon the waters of the stream. "Sequanna," she said, as she tossed the last of the petals, "I pray for the bounty of the hearth. Answer it as you have granted the bounty of the fields."

Linnea settled again upon the woolen cloth. "You must tell me news of the Coritani countryside," said Boudicca, as she licked her fingers from the honeyed glaze of a tiny game bird. Alaina gurgled contentedly as Linnea wrapped her mantle more closely about her as she sat.

"Our harvest brought great bounty this past season," she began. "Our grain was long and golden, and we stored much." She continued, as she pulled a piece of bread from the hearty loaf, adding a slab of cheese. "We keep it safe and guard against the raids of the southern tribes. But," she added, as she drew her legs beneath her, tasting a hearty slab of bread and cheese, "Father says there is unrest among the farmers. There is fear of Roman armies. Word has spread, brought back by our Druids from the isle of Mona."

She paused, taking another slab of the creamy cheese. "It is long that we have told the tales of an evening under the stars and around the hearth of Roman armies last upon our island. Father heard them from his father, and he from his father." She added a slab of bread to the creamy cheese, and then continued. "The Roman armies took the grain of the farmer, and cut down the warrior upon the field of battle. And, worse for some, they took as slaves, to keep them from the glory of the battlefield and the joys of the Otherworld. To cook, to clean, to haul the stones of roads paved for the mounts of Romans, to pull from Roman mines until they dropped the salt of Roman tables."

"Ambiatrix already prepares to lead the field of battle," said Linnea, as she lifted the slab of bread and cheese. "He studies long the pipes of Bibrocus, working the fields as the sun comes up in the sky and piping tunes long after the moon has risen."

"Perhaps Ambiatrix will pipe his tunes for Alaina come Sanheim," said Boudicca, as she gathered the remains of the midday meal to pack again upon the saddle of her mount. "Mandorix has promised a visit to hear me spin the tales of Sanheim." She paused as she rose to place Alaina securely upon the saddle of the chestnut mare. "He has promised Ambiatrix to accompany him, to ride the woodlands and strike the balls of gaming upon Iceni fields."

After they were mounted, they coaxed their mares along the woodland paths, leaving the forest for the meadow, its grasses thick with yellow primroses. They picked up their pace, spurring their mounts to a gallop, the chilled autumn air flying through their tresses as they went, bringing a rise of squeals of glee from Alaina.

On the morrow, Linnea departed for the Coritani fields, with Boudicca accompanying her to the edge of the woodland which stretched below the palace. They embraced as they reached it. Boudicca waved long after her friend spurred her mount to a gallop and rode along the plains into the horizon's mist.

The festival of Sanheim brought Mandorix and Ambiatrix to hear Boudicca's tales. Ambiatrix pleased Alaina with tunes he piped on the silver pipes of an Iceni minstrel, and in turn was pleased by the giggles of the infant.

When the snow of winter came, so came word of a visit from Venutius. The Iberian prince arrived with the chill of northern winds and icicles upon the trees of the Iceni woodlands. He greeted Boudicca with an embrace and greetings from Caractacus. Boudicca stood back to look upon him, his locks and mantle heavy with the snowflakes of a winter storm.

"Oh, Venutius," she said, as she led him down the palace hallways, "you must remove your mantle and come sit by the fire of the great hall. Prasutagus' manservant will dry your mantle by the warmth of a kitchen fire."

Venutius followed, handing his heavy woolen mantle, woven in the hues of the earth on an autumn day, to the waiting servant. "I bring greetings from Caractacus," he said, as he kept pace with Boudicca along the palace floors. "He bids us bring an arrow upon a tree in his place if we ride again the woodland paths, for he has little time spent in idle sport since he has taken the vows of chieftain."

"We shall send it to the center of our target," Boudicca laughed, as she hurried along toward the great hall and the warmth of its many fires. "For Caractacus could bring down the hide of the wildest hare."

Boudicca led Venutius through the entrance of the great hall and to a hassock alongside a blazing fire. Venutius sat upon the hassock, rubbing his hands to bring them warmth, the blaze of the fire bringing a ruddy glow to his usually pale features.

"You must see Alaina," said Boudicca, as she called to a nursemaid to bring the child to her. The nursemaid, carrying the child from play in the nursery chamber, handed her to Boudicca. Alaina laughed with glee, her frame filled out with the passing of a year, as Boudicca placed her upon the clay of the floor. She rose to take a step, falling as soon as she had placed her foot upon the floor, bringing again a rise of her shrieks of laughter.

Venutius beamed upon her, holding his arms out toward her. She rose, her wobbly steps bringing her finally into his outstretched arms. He laughed, and lifted her high, her giggles piercing the quiet of the great hall.

Boudicca called for chestnuts, gathered in the Iceni countryside before the snows of winter, to be brought before them and roasted over the blaze. A kitchen servant appeared, toting a basket full of the gathered nuts, turning them over the open fire until they reached a succulent warmth, breaking them open to serve their tender meat.

Venutius rolled the unroasted nuts along the floor to please Alaina, who chased them with a swift crawl, a pace she kept in her play about the palace.

"You must dine with Prasutagus," said Boudicca to Venutius, as she smiled upon Alaina, "and deliver him the news of the Silures tribe. I shall leave word with kitchen servants to set upon the long tables of the great hall an evening meal fit to renew the spirits after so long a journey." She paused, then continued. "On the morrow, we shall ride the Iceni countryside, to explore its plains and bogs, and to send our arrows toward our marks upon the great trees of the Iceni woodland."

"I shall be delighted to bring news to Prasutagus," returned Venutius. "And, on the morrow, we must be on our mounts come sunrise, for we too shall share our news."

On the morrow, as the sun rose, Boudicca arose to feed Alaina. Then, clad in her sturdiest riding trousers, a woolen tunic and matching mantle woven in the hues of blues of sky and waters, and the greens of springtime meadow grasses, her tresses loose save a length of strands wound back with a tie of coral beads, she made her way to the palace stables. Venutius had arrived, awaiting her presence alongside their mounts, two stallions, their coats brushed to the highest shine, glistening in the rays of the morning sun, their saddles polished and oiled atop blankets of the brightest hues, reds and greens, yellows and blues, pawing the ground in front of them in anticipation of a frisky morning jaunt. Servants cleaned the stalls and threw in fresh hay, and grooms led horses from stalls for an early morning brush, trimming their manes and bringing their coats to a shine.

Venutius greeted Boudicca and called for quivers of arrows to be placed upon their mounts, to try their skill as they wandered through the woodlands. They raced across the meadow, reining in their mounts and laughing to catch their breath as they reached the edge of the forest, the great trunks of its trees rising high with the passing centuries, their flowing branches bare and still with the chill of winter.

As they entered the woodland, they followed the winding paths, sending arrows upon the marks of woodland trees. As hares scurried for cover in their holes behind the rocks of the woodland paths, they divined their tracks as they went, finding favor in their omens.

They lashed their mounts and sat beside a woodland stream, taking their midday meal. The scarlet haws of a hawthorn tree, left dangling by the birds, stood vivid against the barren winter scape and the noise of golden-crested wrens in search of food filled the air about them. As Venutius finished, he sent the small, flat stones he found upon its banks to skim along the rushing waters, skipping downstream as they went.

Venutius spoke. "Boudicca, we must share our news." He paused. "Come Beltane, I shall be joined to Cartimandua. Cunobelinus believes a joining of the Silures and the Brigantes tribes will bode well for both, keeping the southern tribes from raids upon our fields, and strengthening Brigantes borders against the small, fierce tribes of the north."

Venutius paused. "I shall visit still," he continued, "for I shall travel to oversee Brigantes lands and to expand our trade upon the Continent." He quieted, sending a stone upon the rushing waters. "I must listen also for news of the Roman government and its armies, for the Roman emperor Caligula boasts that he has conquered both our island and the Celtic tribes of Germania along the Danube and the Rhine, though he has sent troops against neither."

"It is said that he is mad," he continued, "claiming to be all the Roman gods, felling friends as well as enemies. He rose to emperor currying favor with an aged and desolate Tiberius, himself exiled from Rome, burdened by plots, and opposed by the Roman senate. Caligula knows not the ways of the wise and just Tiberius."

"There are those in Rome," he added, "who have not forgiven the tribes upon our island for aiding the tribes of Gaul as they fought for their freedom against the Roman armies. There are others in Rome," he continued, "who would like to see the Roman empire reach upon our shores as well, to add to the number of slaves who toil in the service of Rome, and to fill still further the overflowing coffers of Rome."

She gazed upon the rushing stream. "I shall be at your rites of joining to wish you well," she said. She paused, then continued. "Come Beltane, another Iceni heir shall fill the palace nursery, for I am again with child."

Venutius paused, splashing the last of his stones upon the icy stream. He lifted Boudicca to stand beside him, drawing the remains of their midday meal into a saddle pouch. They strode to the woodland's edge and unlashed their mounts to climb upon them.

They urged their mounts to a gallop across the meadow, its long brownish grasses broken now only by clumps of aconite and snowdrops. The sun set behind them in brilliant hues of scarlet, mauve, orange and yellow, making way for the crisp and clear starry skies of winter.

Chapter Eight

Come Beltane, chieftains and nobles, merchants and warriors, poured in from almost every island tribe through the gates of the greatest Brigantes city. Festivities reigned, for Cartimandua wished to loosen tongues and soften thoughts, currying the political favor of every inland tribe, and displaying the strength of a Brigantes-Silures union.

To this end, her merchants imported the fruitiest wines from the southern vineyards of Gaul, bringing wagonloads in ships across the sea. Her goat herders gathered milk, turning the softest cheese, and her farmers brought in the grain of their fields to ferment. Her huntsmen brought in the plentiful game of the great Brigantes preserves, smoking it and preserving it beneath the ice of winter waters.

The joining rites began as the moon and the stars rose in the darkened sky. Servants cast the sharpened spikes of torches into the hardened earth of the hillside which sloped beneath the city gates and crowds of guests gathered upon its carefully tended grasses, the hues of their tunics barely visible in the moonlight, their voices already thick with ale.

Cartimandua sat mounted below the hillside, Druids gathered atop it. Her ebony mount, its bright white markings visible on its head and forelegs, was still, held at attention by the head groom of her palace stables. Her silken tunic was scarlet, her tresses in intricate dress bound up with lengths of golden chain. At her signal, a blast of horns was heard about the hillside, and the groom led her mount up the slope.

Venutius followed on foot, flanked on one side by Cunobelinus, his frame bent with age and his step advanced with the aid of a hickory walking stick, his noble head erect with pride. Caractacus flanked him on the other side, his sturdy frame clad in the hues of the Silures tribe, his locks and mustache reddened with the leaves of the henna.

As the Druids gathered, Diviticus was visible among them, his chants and prayers requested by Venutius. His long grey locks shone silver in the moonlight, his long, white robes swayed faintly in the breeze.

As the head Druid Avantes gave the signal to begin, Druid voices filled the air across the night. Justice and peace bestowed on every tribe. A blessing upon this union.

Voices chanted and arms clad in white linen waved about in unison. Ancient prayers issued from the hillside. Ferns and blossoms decked a simple altar, hares and geese in wooden cages above it.

As the voices subsided, the group parted and Diviticus moved to the front. He raised his arms and chanted, "May the Celtic gods bless this union and bring forth from the earth its bounty." Then, he loosed a group of wrens from one of the wooden cages, and intoned his final prayer. "May this union follow the omens of the woodland and the meadow, and bestow upon all the justice of the tribe."

As the crowds began to move about the hillside, Boudicca climbed the slope to search for Votorix and Catrinellia. Her deep, blue tunic, edged with tiny birds and blossoms, its golden belt etched with tiny, Iceni crests, hung on a frame light since the birth of a second Iceni heir. She had named the child Valeda, after a Celtic goddess who brought beauty to the tribes who rained freshly plucked blossoms upon her wooden idol. As she reached the finely-pebbled walkways of the palace grounds, she found Votorix lost in argument over the tactics of war with a retired Brigantes warrior, Catrinellia admiring the blooms of the courtyard, each a speckled orange.

As Votorix spied her, he turned, throwing his arms about her. Then, he stood back, beaming upon her. "How goes the newborn babe?" he asked.

Boudicca smiled, and returned, "She is fine, Papa. And, her tuft of locks looks very much like yours."

At this, Catrinellia moved toward her daughter, alerted by Votorix' booming voice. She embraced her, then stood back to look upon her. "Valeda must learn the royal ways," she reminded her. "And, Alaina is old enough to follow you about. She must begin her royal training."

"Alaina was born with royal ways, Mama," laughed Boudicca. "She orders the servants about and almost always gets her way."

"I have brought her some tiny platters," continued Catrinellia, "etched in silver and gold. She must practice in the nursery."

"And I," said Votorix, "have brought her a dapple-grey pony. She must learn the island countryside."

Boudicca laughed. "I know Alaina will not rest until she and her pony are one about the countryside."

Boudicca embraced them once again and took her leave. As she went, she looked about for Diviticus. As she strolled the hillside, the talk flew all about her. Intertribal justice, raids on tribal grain fields in the dark of night, the new ease of trade upon the Continent, and the gossip of palace halls.

She found Diviticus lost in heavy talk on the interpretation of omens with Avantes and his Brigantes Druids. As she came upon him, he stretched out his arms to wrap her in a great, welcoming embrace, the warmth of his familiar laughter rising above the buzz of the noisy crowd. "It has been long since I have looked upon you, Boudicca," he said, as he stood back. "You must come soon for a chat in the sacred grove."

He took his leave of Avantes and turned to stroll the hillside with Boudicca. "Do you remember the omens we learned and the prayers we chanted beside the sacred stream?" he asked, his great strides visible beneath his long, white robes.

"Oh, yes, Diviticus, I have not forgotten," she answered, as she hastened to keep up with him. "I must send Alaina to you to learn them as well when she is able, and Valeda when she grows to run and climb about."

"I shall soon be very busy," he continued, as they strolled. "Galix, son of Andromatus, has come to me to study the learning of the Druids." He paused, then spoke. "He is very quick and serious. But it will be many years before he stands beside me to perform the ancient rites. He must learn the name of every woodland plant, the magic of its healing, the omens of the birds and woodland creatures, the tales of the stars, and the many chants of the ancient Celtic rites. He must travel, too, to learn the ways of tribal justice." He paused. "My own training," he added, "passed more than twenty Beltanes."

"Will you go to the isle of Mona?" asked Boudicca, puffing slightly in her quest to keep up with Diviticus.

"Yes," he answered. "I shall leave soon to travel north for the Druids' annual gathering."

Diviticus ended his strolling, standing atop a hillside which looked out over the vast Brigantes lands, the blaze of torches beneath them a vivid orange and yellow mist against the starlit sky, its warmth a comfort to the slight chill of the evening. Then, he took his leave, promising Boudicca news of the newly discovered stars and omens, and edicts handed down after long and intense discussion.

Marcus Quintilius Calenus looked over the rail of the Roman warship. The oarsmen, slaves of the Roman empire, pulled fast and furious beneath him. The sails were hoisted, but there was little wind to fill them.

The blue-green waters of the ocean disappeared behind him, only to be replaced by waters of identical hue. The mist of the horizon surrounded the galley ship.

As Marcus stood, he mused upon the follies of youth. He had joined the praetorian guard against his father's wishes, cutting short his schooling and pushing farther into the future the certain comfort of a Roman senator's life.

It was just a few short days ago when he had been standing in the streets of Rome on leave, in counsel with his closest friends, all sons of high-born families. The headiness of ale had loosened their tongues. As the shadows of evening fell about them over the cobbled streets, they argued the merits of their families' slave girls, leaving the matter of where they spent the night to a gold and silver rounded gambling puck.

As they talked, Marcus felt the hand of a praetorian guard fall gently on his shoulder. It was Gaius Lapidus, older and a career soldier, whom he knew very little.

"Marcus," he said, as he stood facing the younger man, "Fabius Antonius has commanded every soldier on leave to return to camp immediately. I will accompany you back to our quarters."

As they walked through the streets of Rome toward the great number of buildings which housed them, Marcus still a bit wobbly on his feet, Gaius Lapidus catching him at intervals, Marcus wondered what news Fabius Antonius, their centurion, had to tell them.

As they assembled upon the field of camp, all roused from their barracks and the streets of Rome, Fabius Antonius, tall, his dark, curly locks falling about his ears, his jagged features hardened from the several campaigns he had spent in the service of Rome, stood before them.

"Our great emperor Claudius, ruler of Rome, has decreed that we finish the job which our great ancestor Julius Caesar set out to accomplish nearly a century ago. The Roman senate has concurred. We must conquer the island of the Britons which lays west of the Roman empire."

He paused, then continued. "Today, we collect very little of the tribute which the few tribes Caesar managed to bow into submission on the island agreed upon, before he was called back again to Gaul. But, the Celtic tribes of the British Isles will be easy to conquer." He paused, letting the effect of his words sink in.

Then, he continued. "Their people are barbaric, with strange customs. They worship their gods at the feet of strange, religious priests, who wave their arms wildly worshiping mistletoe about a flock of sacred geese. In battle, they make strange noises, covering themselves with the blue of the woad plant, and often fighting naked.

"In Caesar's time they aided the cause of Gaul. Now, they stand alone, no Celts left to challenge the Roman empire, save the few along the Danube and the Rhine."

He paused again, then continued. "Their people live simply, in huts with no luxuries and only a loose alliance to a tribal chief. We shall soon be back again on the streets of Rome, the Roman empire richer. Our games will be filled with sport, our tables with the finest wines and sauces, and our evenings with slave girls and chance."

As Fabius Antonius ended his speech, they all filed back into the barracks, spare by the standards of home and the plushness of the taverns and baths, to reflect and to gather together their few possessions into a traveling pack.

Although even the praetorian guard were discouraged from personal possessions, Marcus had saved a few mementos from his many nights in Rome. A golden gambling puck which had brought him luck. A silver stylus inscribed with the name of his closest friend, Lacertian Minucius Vespillo, who lost the writing instrument to Marcus in a game of chance on the night they had first discovered the headiness of ale. He also included a letter he had received from his father on the first night he had joined the praetorian guard. As he re-read the words, he gazed at the boldness of the script.

Dear Marcus,

As you know, I did not agree with your decision to join the praetorian guard. But, the guard is filled with men of courage and honor, the elite of the Roman army, many with the tactical skills which has brought to us for centuries the glory that is Rome. Learn well from them, for many a Roman senator has risen from their ranks, versed in the art of governing the men of Rome.

Your mother sends her good wishes, and your sisters, too. Keep well, my son. May the gods be with you.

Your Father,
Gaius Antonius Calenus

Marcus took a last glance at the letter, its script penned boldly on the finest of writing papers, and tucked it neatly in his traveling pack. Then, he prepared for sleep, for it would be some time he knew before he felt even the comfort of the sparsest barracks bed.

As Marcus reflected on the deck of the galley ship, miles across the Continent from Rome, he remembered Fabius Antonius' words. As a student in one of the finest schools in Rome, tutored by a household slave from Crete, he had learned the history of Rome, the great deeds of Caesar, the glory of the Roman empire. He felt certain his unit would be back in Rome by the Ides of May, nearly a year from now, for his favorite amusement, the annual race of the best charioteers, the winner to be promised freedom, a competition laid out on the grounds of the great Circus Maximus. By then, he mused, he would have enough adventure to earn the respect of his father, regale his sisters with tales of foreign lands, and impress the city's most nubile maidens and slave girls.

As he stood, Lucius Varrus, a career officer, ambled to the side of the deck, leaning over the railing to lose his morning's fare. His curly, dark locks, usually groomed and neat, fell tousled about a face nearly the hue of the sea. As he recovered, he nodded and grinned at Marcus.

"The Roman soldier," he said, as he steadied his feet upon the lurching deck, "faces perils he has not prepared for in training."

Marcus grinned back. "When we reach Londinium, you will lead us in tactical maneuvers."

"Londinium is well fortified," he answered. "Its gates are strong and their stakes are sharply honed. But," he added, as a ruddy hue began to return faintly to his features, "the city and its countryside shall be easy to conquer. Our weapons, our armor, our discipline, and our tactics far surpass those of the Celtic barbarians."

Marcus turned to look again at the sea, picturing the grandest chariot races of the Circus Maximus, and the comrades he would regale there with tales of his wartime adventures.

Chapter Nine

Caractacus sat across the council table from Bellovaci, the Ordoveces chieftain. Ale and honeyed cakes lay on a nearby rough-hewn oaken table, but neither chieftain had touched them.

The great Trinovantes seaport had been sacked by the Roman army, and the remaining tribal cities soon vanquished. Ambiorix, the Trinovantes chieftain, had surrendered to the Roman army and a Roman governor had been set over the Trinovantes lands. Ambiorix had been taken off in chains, along with his closest advisors. The warriors who survived the battle, along with the Trinovantes strongest and most nubile maidens, were shipped to Rome in chains as slaves.

The Duboni to the west stood between the Silures and the approaching Roman army. The Duboni, an inland tribe which had refused to align itself with other Celtic tribes in trade or battle, would almost certainly fall to the Roman army, fresh from victory, its generals carefully trained in the art of tactical battle.

The Belgae to the south were warlike, fighting amongst themselves as well as with most of the island tribes. But, they had paid a price when they had asked for Caesar's help to stave off the Duboni's raids upon their fields nearly a century ago. Their tribute was sent to Rome almost every year, and they had ties to the Roman empire. They would not resist the Roman army.

Caractacus looked at Belovaci before he spoke. The Ordoveces chieftain sat nearly filling his great, oaken chair, his mustache flowing, his blond locks falling beneath his massive shoulders. "Our only hope," began Caractacus, earnestly leaning forward upon his elbows as he spoke, "is joining the forces of our two great tribes."

Belovaci spoke. "I agree," he answered, as he paused in thought. He continued. "I shall call Cotius and Litavacus to ride with you come morning. They shall sit in council with your oldest and best warriors, for they know the strength of the Ordoveces."

"We must also forge the weapons of battle," he continued, as he leaned forward, his elbows upon the rough-hewn timbers of the council table. He paused, then spoke again. "Our artisans are quick to turn out the swords and shields, but they must have the large supply of bronze which favors the Silures lands."

Caractacus agreed. "We must turn out chariots as well, for the Romans fight mounted to match our skills in battle. And helmets," he added, "for the Romans are trained to throw their lances with certain aim."

Belovaci spoke. "You must spend the night among the comforts of the palace," he said, as he rose. "And," he added, as he motioned toward the nearby laden table, "you must take refreshment, for you and your advisors rode long and hard to sit at the council table."

Servants pulled chairs to the low-placed table as the two chiefs settled themselves beside it. Others brought from the larder cheeses and breads as well. As they ate, Caractacus mused on the fate that had brought the two together. Belovaci was the most independent of the island's chieftains, repelling border raids alone with Ordoveces warriors, turning out the supplies of daily life with raw materials found only on Ordoveces lands. He eschewed the politics of festivals and inter-tribal council, keeping peace with the Silures tribe whose lands bordered on the Ordoveces'.

After several long draughts, Belovaci laid his tankard of ale on the table and spoke. "My father and his father were chieftains before me, and my grandfather's father before him. Our warriors have never bent before an attack, even when the Ordoveces tribe was settled along the Danube river."

Caractacus licked his fingers after a hearty slab of bread and cheese and honeyed cakes and ale. "My great grandfather Viridomarus stood against the Roman army when Caesar was pledged to draw our island into the Roman empire." He paused, then spoke again. "His warriors drove off the Romans and aided the conquered tribes of Gaul, sending Caesar fleeing to the Continent to subdue the rebellious tribes."

Bards standing at the ready, gathered before them at Belovaci's signal, pouring forth the tales of ancient Celtic warriors, told to the tunes of minstrel's lyres. The wood of the instruments was turned with the gods and the bounty of the lands, the melodies soothing the weariness of their souls.

As the entertainment ended, Belovaci rose, calling for his advisors to join him at the council table. Caractacus rose as well, heading for the guest chamber set aside for him at his arrival, accompanied by an Ordoveces servant. He must rest, for the return journey to the Silures palace would be hard and quick. The Silures must begin plans at once to thwart the Roman army.

Chapter Ten

Venutius turned his mount toward the sea. Iberia's roads were newly paved with the bricks of Roman ovens, laid by slaves in the toil of the Roman empire. The roads of the countryside were cobbled, the round and uneven stones giving an interesting pattern to a long and sometimes winding way, stones pulled and sorted as they stopped a farmer's plow.

In the two years since he had been made emperor of Rome, Claudius had restored order to the Roman empire. His newly restructured government had brought roads to the remotest of provinces, efficiently piped water to their greatest cities, and a great port to the city of Rome. Now, it was time to take the only unconquered land that lay west of the Roman empire.

Venutius slowed his mount to a trot. He would board a ship headed north, as soon as he was able to complete the necessary transactions to commission one. The sun felt warm upon his back and his gaze fell upon the great expanse of passing Iberian vineyards. Occasionally, the lushness of silvery olive groves replaced them.

As he urged along his mount, he mused on the mission which had brought him to Iberia. He had opened new trade routes for a variety of the best Brigantes goods. Cartimandua would be pleased, for daily she cajoled her artisans to increase their quotas, threatening, pleading, and promising rewards. Her efforts had paid off, bringing from the Continent the finest wines, first press oils, the most delicately spun silks from the east, and the most highly developed pungent scents she valued.

Venutius had also visited his family in their tiny villa. Placed far out into the countryside, it gave his father an advantage as he made his rounds as head tax collector for his provincial district. He was not too far from any Roman subject who failed to provide the full tax assessed upon his person.

As Venutius had approached the villa, dismounting as he handed the reins to a stable servant, he noticed his father working late, seated on the portico, a sheaf of papyrus and stylus strewn across a small, low table, a candle next to it in the moonlight. As he saw Venutius, a smile burst upon his face, creased and worn beneath his thinning locks of grey. His body, heavy and settled, took on for the moment a flicker of his former youth. He rose to greet his son.

As he stood, a youthful version of the man, similar in features but slenderer in frame, bolted from the front entranceway, dashing past him to take the steps of the portico in one leap. Venutius laughed as the youth ran toward him, his arms outstretched, the newly acquired length of his slender legs bolstering his strides as he crossed the neatly clipped green which ran the length of the villa. Epidorix, once the pesky, younger brother who had followed Venutius everywhere about, had grown into a graceful and agile youth. As they embraced, their mingled laughter blotted out the void of the passing seasons, and brought to them both the memories of play they once shared about the villa.

Venutius stood back to look upon his brother. "Epidorix," he said, the gaze of the youth now full in line with his, above a stubble of growth newly sprung about his chin, "you have grown too tall and too swift for me to chase and catch."

"And, you," said Epidorix, eyeing the doeskin breeches and the scabbard about the waist, "have grown into a man."

Then, the two walked toward the portico, Epidorix chattering away, his arms still entwined about Venutius, to embrace their father. Erithrominus silently placed his arms about his eldest son. The gesture brought back memories of the past. The years of the father riding into the countryside, accompanied by his son. The cajoling, the sympathizing, the resentment of a peasant asked to part with crops after long toil which would barely feed his family. And, during rare but occasional leisure, lessons in fishing and catching game, though there were servants to land and place fare upon the family table.

"Now," said Erithrominus, "we must find your mother. All she talks of to those who will listen is the importance of her eldest son to Celtic tradition and his place in the greatest of island tribes." Venutius knew the importance to his mother of his place in the house of Cunobelinus and of his present alliance. Her grandfather, before the Roman rule, had been a Celtic chieftain. Erithrominus led Venutius through the small, front entranceway into the simple vestibule, through the atrium, and out onto the open courtyard. His mother Lillia was instructing a servant by moonlight the place of a sapling fig tree.

As Lillia spied Venutius, her sandaled feet remained fixed on the elaborate tile. Her eyes, always the changing green-blue hue of the open sea, filled with tears. As she recovered, she rushed toward Venutius, her tresses dressed in proper Roman style spilling loose from their clasps, her deep auburn locks now mixed with strands of grey.

As she reached him, she clung to Venutius, the joy of her grasp wiping out the pain of the distance of many passed seasons. She stood back to look upon him. "Venutius," she said, "you have grown into a handsome Celtic warrior. The strength of your alliance has brought us the greatest pleasure."

"We must prepare for you a feast of welcome," she continued. "But, first you must go off with Epidorix, for I can see by his features he must tell you all he has kept to himself for many seasons." Her laughter, the first of the evening, filled the open courtyard.

Venutius embraced his father, bending gently down to kiss his mother upon her cheek. "I will have Epidorix at table with the first summons of a kitchen servant," he promised, as he followed the youth out of the courtyard and into the atrium of the villa.

Epidorix led Venutius to a chamber at the far end of a hall. Roman gods looked down upon the sparsely furnished room and a likeness of the emperor Claudius perched upon an oaken chest. Epidorix lifted the lid, removing from beneath a layer of mantles a rusted sword. Carefully, he held it out to Venutius. "You must teach me all you have learned in study with the warriors and guardians of the Silures palace," he said.

Venutius looked upon the face of his younger brother, the longing of youth impatiently upon it. "It is with pain of death that you lift a sword in your own defense," he said. "For a Celtic Roman subject may wield a weapon only as conscript of the Roman army."

"I know," returned Epidorix. "But, how must I face our ancestors of the Other World?"

Venutius took the sword from his brother's hands. "We must go far into the countryside," he said, "for even the servants must not know our mission." As Venutius laid the rusted weapon back beneath the layer of mantles, he added, "On the morrow, we must both be at the stables before the first rays of the early morning sun."

True to their pact, as the rays of the morning's sun set upon the servants' quarters, the brothers were headed toward a secluded woodland, one of the few left untilled about the plateau of arable Iberian countryside, its greenery set in the middle of a rocky, barren landscape. As they lashed their mounts to a hickory, Epidorix pulled from his saddlebag the rusted sword. "We must make haste," said Venutius, as he pulled from a scabbard hitched about his waist the bronze of a carefully burnished sword. "Mother and Father will miss us as the sun rises farther toward midday."

The agility of Epidorix and the patience of Venutius brought quickly to Epidorix the skill of the sword. As the brothers increased their visits to the woodland, Epidorix' footwork began to match more carefully the movements of his sword. "You must come here often after I'm gone," said Venutius. "With practice, you will match the skills of the bravest Celtic warrior." After they finished, they often rode back in silence, each savoring the companionship of the other, or chatted until the sun went down.

Activity filled the days with Lillia and Erithrominus. Lillia was content to sit and gaze upon her son, offering him the delicacies of their frugal larder. Or pulling him about to show him her latest culinary improvement or addition to the courtyard garden. Erithrominus, though slower in his rounds, insisted Venutius accompany him on them, stopping occasionally to chase a fish, swift in the sparkle of a slowly meandering stream.

Or to talk of politics. The rumors he heard from the Roman officials as they claimed the taxes he collected. The whispers and boasts that Claudius would take the last of the Celtic holdouts, the isle where Caesar had a century ago forged but a loose alliance.

As the rays of the sun grew shorter, Venutius packed his traveling bags, adding to them a shirt given him by his mother embroidered with her grandfather's tribal crest, a wooden figure of a naked Celtic warrior carved by Epidorix on rests during their jousting sessions, and a small, leather pouch from Erithrominus, tooled about with the crest of the Celtic tribe in which legacy named him chief before the Roman rule.

As Venutius mused upon the memories of his visit, he spied a ship which would hold both man and mount. Standing upon its deck to pay his passage, he savored the sun upon his back. The black clouds of storm were already forming out over the open sea.

Chapter Eleven

Boudicca awaited Venutius in their favored grove in the woodlands which stretched below the Iceni palace. She had brought with her some tiny, honeyed game, slabs of ripened cheese and the warmth of a newly-turned out bread, the freshest goat's milk and a slightly heady mead to enjoy for their midday meal. The choicest fruit hung on a nearby apple tree.

Under its ancient branches and along its gnarled roots, Alaina and Valeda laughed and played, tossing mossy leaves to a brown, speckled hare, and chasing the woodland squirrels. They dangled their toes and threw pebbles into a brook, its slippery stones turned smooth by the centuries' rushing waters. Their mounts were lashed nearby.

Boudicca sat on a linen cloth, its hues mingling the tints of the sunset sky and the blossoms of a springtime meadow. The scent of pink campion wafted about and the chatter of birds gorging themselves on the red and purple berries of the elder and hawthorn trees pierced the chill of the autumn air. Pheasants and partridges scurried for cover as a short burst of wind rained leaves upon their paths. Squirrels shook the branches of a beechmast tree in their quest for winter bounty. The orange and yellow of a newly-burst mushroom contrasted the woodland floor and the trees rose with a blaze of autumn color, the deep, golden yellow of the elm, the gold of the birch, and the golden red of the maple.

As she sat, Boudicca sang tunes and told the tales of ancient Celtic deeds, drawing about her Alaina and Valeda. She sang to them of Etana, a goddess turned into a swan. She sang of Proteus, a mortal youth who pleased the giant god Futan with a brush of bristles for his unruly locks which he plucked from a magical boar, winning his favor and the endless bounty of the streams the god watched over. She sang of the Otherworld, of its trees of silver and gold with leaves of purple crystal, where the purest love reigns free of duty, where sunlight plays and the birds sing softly forever.

Four years had passed since Venutius had been joined to Cartimandua. Since that time, the Brigantes prince consort had often been a welcome visitor in the Iceni palace, joining Prasutagus for stately talks and Boudicca for idylls in the woodlands, accompanied by Alaina and Valeda. Occasionally, as the children played or slept, watched over by their nursemaids, the two would practice their skills of mount together, riding far into the woodlands, across the fields and through the dangerous fens, the memories of their youth alive within them.

As Boudicca sat regaling her children with the wonders of the past, the clap of a horse's hooves against a pine-strewn path cut through the gaiety of their reverie. Venutius appeared, his long, dark locks entangled about a ruddy face newly-etched by the chill of the autumn wind. He dismounted, lashing his sturdy roan to a nearby stand of elders.

"Venutius, Venutius," shouted Alaina, as she ran, her legs sturdy and swift beneath her, her arms outstretched, toward the

Brigantes prince. Valeda followed, her legs still chubby, straining to match the pace of her swifter sister.

Venutius chuckled, as he bent to wrap his outstretched arms about them, lifting them as one into the air. "What do you have for me?" asked Venutius, holding them aloft beneath the elders. "I have five kisses and hugs," said Alaina. "One from my pony Nerthus, and four from my pet turtles I have collected from the woodland." Venutius laughed as Alaina hugged and kissed him, Valeda giggling as she tried to do the same.

"Now, let's see what I have for you," he said, as he set them softly down upon the shaded grasses of the clearing. He reached into his traveling pack, its tooled scrolls surrounding a Brigantes seal. He pulled from it a carefully carved doll, chiseled with a summer tunic. A band of blossoms hung about its neck. He handed it to Alaina. And for Valeda, a ball, carved from the wood of an oak fallen by a camp site.

As Alaina took the doll, she quieted, struck by the image which looked very much like her. Then, she hoisted it upon her shoulders, running about to show it the woodland flowers, calling each by name. Valeda, quickly taken by her new toy, rolled the ball about the mossy woodland, aiming for a stand of elders, and shrieking with joy whenever the width of a trunk stopped the rounded, wooden object.

Then, Venutius, weary from his journey, knelt beside Boudicca, arranging his lanky frame to lean against a great, red maple. As they sat, he plucked a blade of grass, blowing into it to raise a tune to entertain the children.

As the chill of the autumn wind swirled about them, carrying with it the slight fragrances of the crabapple and elderberry tree, Venutius related the tales of his journey to Boudicca. His visit to the villa of Erithrominus. Newly-paved roads which ran into the countryside, bringing upon them tax collectors directly from the streets of Rome. Water, brought by pipes, even to the remotest province, to irrigate figs and olives, grapes and grain, raised on land once left untilled, to grace the Roman tables. And, great temples, raised by the labor of slaves, with altars to worship the Roman gods, watched over by stony images of Claudius.

As the children played, the two talked idly of their ambitions and dreams. Of Venutius' plans to organize and distribute fairly the lands of Brigantes nobles, keeping peace among them. Of Boudicca's plans to liven the palace meals with music of the bards and to add to the hues of the palace chambers with sprays of woodland flowers. And, her plans to raise Alaina and Valeda with charity and fun as well as duty.

Together, they walked the woodland floor, gathering hickory nuts and splashing in a narrow stream, Venutius snatching a speckled trout to add to their evening table. As they walked, Venutius spoke. "I must return soon to the Brigantes palace, for Cartimandua is impatient to increase her output of trade," he said. He stopped, reaching out to pluck a woodland rose and handing it to Boudicca, who placed it in the single, deep-green linen tie that held her long, red tresses. She giggled as they crossed a stream, lifting her tunic to save a drenching of its gracefully embroidered edges.

He continued. "I must also send word to Caractacus of the whispers about the Continent of Claudius' plans to set his army upon the shores of our isle," he added. "And, I must talk to Prasutagus."

As the sun began to set, and the children grew sleepy with play, they packed their linens and pulled the two princesses onto their own mounts, leading Alaina's pony behind them. There would just be time for Venutius to wash off the dust of his journey. Boudicca had left word with the kitchen servants to set out plenty of wine and ale, delicately roasted birds, and wild boars well-turned upon the spit, for she knew Venutius and Prasutagus would talk far into the night.

Chapter Twelve

Caractacus stood upon a hill overlooking the great Trevari River. Woodlands stretched behind.

Seven Beltanes had passed since Londinium had been toppled, prey to a well-trained Roman army. Two seasons later, moving west to lay waste to every small tribe in its path, taking hostages and booty, it had reached the Silures lands.

Cartimandua, eager to save the trade routes which had for so long brought her the luxuries she adored, on the fall of Londinium quickly claimed herself a friend of the Roman Empire. Prasutagus, in an effort to forestall the decimation of the Iceni tribe, and to protect its great wealth, became a client-king, forging an agreement with Rome for independent rule.

Caractacus had persuaded Belovaci, the chieftain of the Ordoveces tribe to the north, and long the most fiercely independent chieftain of the isle, to join his warriors to the Silures in a stand against the Roman army. He had swelled their numbers with the Suebi and the Ubii, Celts from along the Danube and the Rhine, who asked very little to enter the field of battle, a sack of grain or a tin bowl or two turned out by an island artisan, whose tribes discouraged the ownership of lands or coin, prizing only valor, and who had succeeded in repelling every attempted Roman invasion of their borders.

Belovaci had agreed as well to forge the weapons of traditional Celtic battle. Chariots to scatter the enemy, picking up and dropping off the warriors of a skirmish. Shields the size of a warrior's frame. Helmets with likenesses of animals and horns atop, giving courage to the warrior and fright to his enemy challenger. Extra-long javelins and spears.

Caractacus chose the woodlands to make camp, issuing orders to both the Silures and the Ordoveces, to make haste. All must be hidden by sundown, laying in wait for a surprise attack when the enemy appeared. He also ordered the hills to be fortified with rocks along their slopes, impeding an easy ascent by the advancing Roman army.

As the work progressed, Caractacus retired to the woodland, checking the points where his warriors must hide to best be out of sight. His warriors, greatly outnumbered, had kept the Romans at bay by fighting fiercely, retreating, and fighting fiercely again. But, the Roman army was regularly replenished with troops from Rome, fortified by a lengthy military tradition. His warriors, long without women, home, and children, and watching their neighbors succumb to the Roman sword, were quickly fatiguing. They needed a victory to raise morale.

To this end, Caractacus went about, encouraging, admonishing, and cajoling. Pointing out that victory meant freedom, defeat the loss of their women and a life of slavery at the hands of Rome. His warriors, many of them barely on the horizon of youth, were busy covering their naked frames with the deep-blue dye of the woad plant, a tactic which always startled the enemy and gave courage to the user.

As soon as Caractacus was satisfied his warriors understood his plan, he retired to a clearing behind a stand of elms, gathering his advisors as he went. They settled informally, kneeling in a circle behind the trees. The first to speak was Epidoris, a youth of long, blond locks turned nearly white by the rays of the sun, his pale, blue eyes reflecting the shyness of a youth who had longed to study the Druid ways.

As a child, he had adored the animals of the woodland, playing often with the sacred hare and the goose. Now, he was using the secrets of the woodland, hovering unseen about the Roman camp, bringing back news he observed or overheard.

"The Romans plan to break camp at dawn," said Epidoris, "marching toward the hills of our palace city. They carry many provisions, for they plundered the corn and grain left by our farmers as they hurried toward the safety of our city gates."

He paused, then continued. "They bring warriors on mount as well as on foot," he said. "Their arms are polished and honed, for they bring with them many slaves from the tribes which they have laid waste since the conquest of Londinium."

Caractacus leaned forward, waiting until Epidoris was still. "They must pass between the river and the woods," he said. "The river is deep, and they will not be able to cross."

"We will drive those on foot toward the slope of the river's banks," he added. "The heavy iron that covers the Roman warrior will send those who bear it to the bottom of the Treveri River."

"Those on mount we will drive to the fen beyond the woodland," he continued. "The deep bogs of the fen will catch the hooves of their mounts, driving their warriors to their feet to meet the Celtic sword.

On the morrow, a group of our warriors will creep forward covered by boughs, pushing the Romans towards the river's edge. As they pass, we will challenge them in battle, circling around to cut off their mounted aid."

The lines of weariness were carefully etched about Caractacus' deep, blue eyes, now visible in the moonlight, once asparkle on carefree woodland jaunts. "Our warriors must slumber well tonight," he said. "We will send our best youths out to keep watch from the boughs of the woodland treetops. The full moon lights the plains below through which the Romans must pass."

As Caractacus finished, he dismissed his advisors, admonishing them to be sure to take their share of rations. Grain supplied by their farmers and hurriedly baked into bread over an open camp fire, birds brought down by the skill of the bow, and bigger game brought in from the woodland, renewing their strength for battle.

Then, he crossed the grassy plain, trodding the hillside to the river's banks. Moonbeams bobbed along its rushing waters, swollen from a fortnight of rain. A speckled trout, visible in the moonlight, made its way downstream. A hickory tree, its bare branches awaiting the renewal of spring, stood nearby, its ancient roots protruding along the lush riverbank.

Caractacus mused upon the morrow's battle, measuring the height of the river. Then, he returned to the woodland, checking to make sure his warriors were all bedded down for the night. He saved his words of prodding and encouragement for the morrow.

As he settled upon a bedding of his own, on boughs laid down upon the mossy, woodland floor, amidst a spate of fading, autumn blossoms, he thought of Cortitiana. She would now be putting the children into their beds, their chambers filled with the toys of childhood, her soft voice singing them the lullabies of their ancestors.

Caractacus stared at the clear, dark sky, studded with stars, visible between the treetops. He hoped that the ancient warrior Valarian, who he had left behind to ward off raiders and keep the bulwarks of the city intact, would put to good use the services of the farmers who had fled their fields for the safety of its gates. Then, as he mused once again on the plans of battle for the morrow, and searched the sky for the stars which had so often guided his journeys, weariness forced him into a fitful slumber.

Chapter Thirteen

Dawn broke the ebon of the cold, dark sky with a burst of violet rays backed by an orange-red sun. A group of Silures warriors, covered by boughs, inched forward. Horn blowers, many of them the bards and vates of the palace, stood behind, the wood of their instruments turned with the reeds and the holes which would make the deepest and loudest sounds.

Chariots stood at the ready, hidden behind the stands of trees. Warriors, their shaved bodies glistening in the sun, many naked, many covered with the blue dye of the woad plant, stood hidden as well.

The chatter of birds was all that broke the silence. Caractacus, ready to lead his men into battle with the Romans, stood at the rear of a chariot, the reins of a horse decked out in enameled harness, its bridle and bit of the finest leather and bronze, in the hands of a long-trusted driver.

Caractacus wore the heavy torque of a chieftain, encircled with the gods of the Silures tribe. His helmet was topped with a likeness of the horns of the woodland stag. His tunic was closed with a girdle of gold embedded with Silures crests.

The noise of the advancing army's footsteps preceded its arrival at the foot of the hill which led to the narrow, grassy plain which passed between the river and the woodland. Quiet pervaded the woodland, save for the calls of the blackbirds and finches, and the scattering of the squirrels along its branches.

The Romans traveled in close formation, the armor which covered them identical. Helmets topped by a bright, red crest, a tooled, leather breastplate, and a shield sporting the crest of Rome. As they reached the crest of the hill, the Celtic warriors covered by boughs moved forward to charge their front lines. The bards and vates set up a blare with their horns. Chariots rushed from the woodland to rain javelins upon the legion, their clattering wheels adding to the din. Warriors dropped from the chariots to fight the Romans on foot, others emerging from the woodland as well.

As the chariots retired to the sidelines, chaos replaced the order of the Roman legions. Foot soldiers scattered in fear and in confusion. Weighed down by their armor and their traveling packs, the Romans were at a disadvantage in the hand-to-hand combat with the unencumbered Celtic warriors. But, the Celts, despite the superior length of their well-turned javelins and swords, the boost they got by the element of surprise, and the ferocity of their battle skills, were outnumbered. The Romans, recovered from their confusion, often fended off the blows of a single Celtic warrior with a line of shields placed side to side.

As the wounded Celts were carried off by the waiting chariots, and replaced by fresher warriors, the Romans were spurred in their combat by the lure of the beauty and strength of the glistening bodies of the naked, Celtic warriors, who they hoped to turn into slaves.

As the Celts drove the Romans, still weighted down by their traveling packs and armor, toward the river, the Roman's mounted units arrived, alerted by the sounds of battle. Bolstered by the confusion, Caractacus, standing tall in the rear of his chariot, rushed from the woodland, followed by the rest of the chariots holding many Celtic warriors. The Roman horsemen, recognizing the trappings of a chieftain, gave chase. The Celts, headed for the fens, with their superior skills of mount, and knowledge of the countryside, reached the bogs before the Romans, pulling their chariots to the side and bringing them to a halt. But, the Romans, caught up in the excitement of the chase, pulled too late upon the reins of their mounts, the hooves of their horses slipping and sinking in the unsure footing of the marshy bog.

The Celts jumped from their chariots to face the Roman horsemen, most thrown to the floating logs and reeds of the fen, many a victim of the hooves of a frightened, screeching mount. The rest had difficulty gaining a foothold themselves. Those who made it to the edge of the bog faced a waiting, Celtic sword.

Caractacus, who had remained in his chariot, gave orders to the driver to return to the grassy plain above the river. Battle raged along its banks. He rode back and forth above it, calling out, prodding and encouraging, occasionally fending off an enemy sword which sought to topple him from the height of his chariot.

He returned to the fens, where Roman soldiers had gained a footing on the solid ground around it. The Celts fought fiercely, but the sheer numbers of the Roman soldiers, who by now had remembered their tactical training, and had gathered their forces into a more cohesive group, wore down even the bravest warriors.

Caractacus returned to the river, where the Romans were driving the Celts up the hillside and onto the grassy plain for a more equal footing. The riverbank was littered with Roman soldiers and Celtic warriors who had failed to repel an enemy sword. Epidoris, his long, blond locks now matted with the mud of the hillside, was among them. Caractacus restrained himself from jumping into the fray to uncover the Roman soldier who took from the youth his hope of studying to become a Druid.

As the tide of battle turned in favor of the Romans, Caractacus charged the field to gather up two of his most trusted advisors, Belorix and Casivelanus, pulling them into his chariot, and ordering his driver to return to the depths of the woodland, where the enemy would take long to follow on foot. As they reached the middle of the forest, they disembarked, gathering about in a circle. Belorix spoke. "Caractacus," he said, leaning forward slightly toward the Silures chief, "you must flee. If you are taken captive, you will be dragged through the streets of Rome in chains, a trophy before the people, and then sent to the Roman gallows. Without a leader, our warriors will lose desire for battle.

"If you return to battle now, and are felled by the Roman sword, our warriors will be thrown into confusion. You must flee to the safety of the Brigantes palace and of Venutius. From there you will be able to send the orders and plans of battle."

Casivelanus spoke next. "Lucterius will take charge of the Silures and Ordoveces. Thoughts of your safety will settle our warriors and spur them on, giving them strength and courage to face the enemy sword.

"You must travel by the light of the stars, and make camp deep within the woodlands by day, for Roman units wander about the countryside, foraging for the ripened grain and corn."

Caractacus agreed, giving an assent with the raising of his arm. "I will travel alone," he said, as he shifted his stance upon the woodland floor, "lest I arouse suspicion and call attention to a traveling band."

The Silures king rose, giving a few last orders to tide over his warriors until the light of the moon replaced the fading sun. He bid the two advisors farewell, clasping them closely in his great embrace. Then, he gathered up a few supplies, a bow and a quiver of arrows to bring down small game, and several loaves of bread, laying them in his traveling pack, and waited for the first hint of a starlit night.

Chapter Fourteen

As the stars rose, and battle had ceased for the night, Caractacus had two young warriors create a diversion. A drunken brawl, backed by the aid of drunken friends to cheer them on, ensued. The Roman scouts, entranced by the outcome, were drawn to the contest staged upon the riverbank, peering from around the trees they had crept behind.

The moon, merely a sliver, and the cloudy sky, provided the cover Caractacus needed to steal softly away from out the other side of the woods. Familiar with the countryside, and clad only in a simple tunic and mantle, he led his mount slowly and quietly away, down the hillside that had brought the Romans to them, climbing his mount only after he reached a thicket several miles away.

From there, clear of the enemy camp, he rode as far and as hard as he could to put distance between them. Then, he rested his mount, leading it to a nearby stream. As he remounted the chestnut stallion, now refreshed, he checked the stars overhead. Through the cloudy sky, he saw barely the star he needed to follow, by Diviticus' calculations, which would lead him northward. He rode on in its direction.

As he went, he avoided the settlements which had once sheltered his people, lest there be stray bands of Romans roaming about for booty or ripening grain. He traveled until the sun came up, then made camp in the vastness of a woodland.

In this fashion, he traveled northeast, using the green twigs of a sapling to roast a fish he had caught in the moonlight over an open fire, or bringing down a woodland hare for his supper. As he reached the edge of Brigantes lands, he picked up his pace, traveling by day as well as night. The Brigantes peasants provided him with food and water, inviting him to sit around their evening campfires, or dine with them on the compact, dirt floors of their huts.

As they shared with him flagons of ale and the cheeses of their farmsteads, they also shared with him tales of the Roman invaders. Few Romans were seen about the Brigantes countryside, for Cartimandua had chosen to keep order and collect the taxes herself, eagerly turning them over to the Roman empire, leaving the Romans free to vanquish other tribes. Farmers still sowed their grain, for unlike the neighboring tribes who had resisted Roman domination, and had been decimated by the taking of slaves and booty, leaving no young hands to plow the furrows or lead a band of cattle to pasture, the Brigantes farmers were still able to raise their cattle, keep their farmstead goats, and turn their grain into ale.

But, woodland game no longer filled the cauldrons of their evening meals, for arms were forbidden, to be raised only in the aid of a Roman conflict. And, though the revelry of Beltane and Sanheim still marked the seasons of planting and of harvest, there were no contests of valor.

The white hare still ran free, but no longer was brought to the altar of religious woodland rites, for the Druids, long prey to the vagaries of the Roman empire, and annihilated in the conquest of the Continent's Celtic tribes a century before, had fled to the Isle of Mona. The rivers still flowed and the earth still stretched before them, but the Brigantes, toiling to produce the heavy taxes levied upon them, seldom worshiped the goddesses they once believed watched over them.

Caractacus, renewed by the fare and the respite of the Brigantes people, moved on to reach the palace city at Sanheim. As he identified himself, and the gates of the city were swung open, he rode down the narrow, winding streets toward the luxury of the sprawling palace. Refusing the hospitality of a bath or slumber, he asked to be taken directly to the Brigantes queen.

Announced by a servant, and led to the great hall where Cartimandua held court, he stepped before her. Cartimandua, meeting his gaze, showed no sign of recognition. Caractacus spoke. "I have come to see Venutius," he said, "and to take refuge within these gates. To command my warriors from the safety of great distance."

Cartimandua spoke, her steely gaze unmoving. "Venutius has ridden south to mediate a dispute between two landowners," she said. "Our Druids, unmindful of the tasks for which we have fed them and given them shelter, have fled to the Isle of Mona. Their cowardice has increased the duties of Venutius."

"I ask only for simple hospitality," returned Caractacus, "and messengers to carry my orders to the Silures warriors."

"How goes your quarrel with the Roman empire," asked Cartimandua.

"We have battled steadily for seven seasons," he answered. "We have driven back the Romans, but they advance, adding often fresh troops from the barracks of Rome."

Cartimandua spoke again. "As you know," she said, "I have aligned myself with the Roman empire."

"I have heard the news," he answered. "But, surely your heritage and the memory of your father disagrees."

At that, a sneer crept across Cartimandua's steely countenance. "My father," she returned, "has long been valiant in the Otherworld. I rest here, my palace well provided for, our city prosperous." She paused, then continued. "I have made a treaty with the Romans to keep order within the borders of Brigantes lands, and to harbor no enemy of the Roman empire."

"But, Cartimandua," said Caractacus, his gaze now fully upon her, "ours has been a friendship of childhood. We have wandered the woodlands together, bringing down game for an evening supper. You have taken as consort a prince raised as my brother under my father's roof."

"I have no sentiment for the days of yore," she answered.

"Then," he said, "I will have to wait for Venutius to return and deliver his opinion on the matter."

With a flick of her wrist, Cartimandua ordered two palace guards to seize him. Caractacus pulled free, but several more surrounded him as well.

"Throw him in chains," she commanded. "And, prepare him to be delivered to the Roman empire."

Chapter Fifteen

Caractacus, weighed down by the chains that bound him, sat tall in the carriage that brought up the rear of the procession that was winding down the streets of Rome. Cortitiana, in the carriage ahead, surrounded by their children, all bound, and pale and trembling, comforted them as she could.

Women and children lined the streets, as well as heads of households. Boys, let out by their Greek slave tutors from their lessons jostled for position, anxious to catch a glimpse of the Celtic chief whose deeds had been for seven years on the tongues of all their elders.

The spectacle, grand even by Roman standards, did not disappoint. The praetorian guard, decked out in full regalia, headed the procession, followed by carriages of booty vanquished from the Silures palace. Torques heavy with gold, drinking vessels and urns of bronze, and trinkets of every kind, many of them studded with the pink and red coral of the sea.

Next came the servants of the Silures palace, all bound and on foot, shuffling as best they could and occasionally prodded by guards, to keep up with the carriages before them. As the procession wound down, it stopped in front of a throne set for

Claudius aside of the army's barracks, where the emperor sat surrounded by his tribunes. Agrippina, his wife, sat on a throne beside him.

As the carriages were brought to a halt, Caractacus was placed before the emperor's throne. But, unlike the captive kings before him, who had always bowed to the Roman victors, the Silures king remained erect.

Caractacus addressed Claudius. "Had I been as equal to you in wealth as in noble birth, I would have entered your city as friend instead of captive. I had warriors and horses, arms and wealth. What wonder if I parted with them reluctantly?

"If you Romans choose to lord it over the world, does it follow that the world is to accept slavery? Were I to have been at once delivered up as prisoner, neither my fall or your triumph would have become famous. My punishment would be followed by oblivion. But, if you save my life, I shall be an everlasting memorial of your clemency."

Claudius looked upon Caractacus, the chieftain's gaze unflinching, despite the weight of his shackles. The emperor spoke. "What you say is true. I shall spare your life." He paused, shifting his gaze slightly toward Agrippina, who nodded. "But," he continued, "you must live within the confines of Rome, a symbol of my great generosity toward your barbarian people."

At that, Claudius granted pardon to the Silures king, and to his wife and children. He motioned for them to be released from their bonds. As soon as they were free, they knelt before him, praising him for his generosity. Then, they bowed before Agrippina with similar words of praise.

Then, the senate put forth its finest orators, who agreed that the triumph matched the capture of the greatest enemy kings in the history of Rome. Special awards and privileges were granted to Ostorius, the general who had led the latest campaigns against the Silures tribe.

Caractacus was given a villa in Rome, and tutors for his sons, an education equal to the highest born. But, guards were posted to keep the family within the city's limits.

As he wandered the well-cobbled streets of Rome, his once sturdy frame turned soft, his days spent in the idleness of the daily tasks of the Roman citizens about him, the Silures chieftain wondered, often aloud, what Rome had ever wanted with the small huts of the British Celts.

Chapter Sixteen

Venutius, worn from his journeys about the southern countryside of Brigantes lands, handed the reins of his mount to a palace stable servant. Then, he headed across the courtyard, treading the stone pathways that led along the manicured gardens, toward a small, side door which opened onto a corridor that led to the sleeping chambers and the bathing chambers which held great iron footed tubs. But, as he passed the great hall, a shrill voice calling out his name kept him from pursuit of respite.

"Venutius, I see your return has remained unannounced," said Cartimandua, her loud, hoarse voice carrying to the hallway. "But do come in and tell me about your journey."

Venutius obliged, entering the great hall and handing his mantle to a waiting servant. Cartimandua spoke again. "Sit by my feet," she said, motioning to a nearby stool, "and tell me about the outcome of your travel."

Venutius pulled the stool toward the oaken chair where Cartimandua sat and settled himself upon it. "Order has been restored in the southern countryside," he began. "I have enlisted the help of Laertissmus, the noble who oversees the greatest amount of lands. He knows well the problems of the nobles who are his neighbors."

"The ban on arms has taken a toll on the farmers' morale," he continued. "Unable to quickly ward off raiders, they watch their fields at night but, though some have mounts equal to the chase, they are unable to stop all those who decide to pilfer."

"The heavy taxes have brought an increase in the amount of grain they are expected to yield," he continued. "The nobles, knowing the grain they must send on the ships to Rome, push the farmers harder, and fight among themselves over the land."

"What was your decision?" asked Cartimandua, maintaining an interest despite an icy countenance.

"We expanded the farmers' fields, bringing together the resources of every noble, and increased the nighttime guards, banding together the area farmers and the servants of the nobles. The duty has brought together the neighbors of the south, who now share gossip as well as flagons of ale."

Venutius paused. "I often wish that we could have stood against the Romans," he continued, "then have turned to do their bidding."

Cartimandua's sloe-green eyes began to narrow. "Venutius," she returned, "that is my decision to make. You are merely a consort to Brigantes royalty." Venutius answered. "I was trained under the roof of a chief whose heir has stood against the Romans with great courage. His name has brought fear to every Roman general."

Cartimandua smiled. "Rome has no fear from Caractacus now," she responded. "While you were gone, he sought refuge within our gates. I sent him upon the galleys of the Romans, to be brought before Claudius to decide his fate."

At that, Venutius jumped from the stool, meeting Cartimandua's gaze. "How could you deliver a childhood friend who showed only the courage of his ancestors to the Roman enemy?" he demanded.

"I am queen," she answered. "I have final command. And," she continued, "I am indebted to our Roman friends."

Cartimandua raised her hand to dismiss Venutius. "I must continue with the business of the day," she said.

"You are no longer my queen," he answered, "and you shall feel my wrath. For I will avenge Caractacus' fate."

Dismissing the quarrel as one of many the two had often had, Cartimandua turned to her closest advisors, launching into a discussion of the affairs of state.

Venutius turned to leave the great hall, treading the corridors toward a footed, cast iron tub to soak the dust of his journey off. As he ran the course soap, scented with mulberry, along his frame, turned lean and sinewy with his many jaunts about the countryside, he thought only of the swords he had laid aside since Roman rule.

Chapter Seventeen

Venutius stood on the plains of the southern Brigantes countryside, on lands he had helped to fairly dispense. Grain grew all around him, the lowing of milk cows a distant hum upon the wind.

He had gathered about him a ragtag band of warriors, its numbers swelling as it moved north to challenge the palace city. Lords and farmers, Silures warriors bent on avenging Caractacus' fate, and a healthy addition of warriors from along the Danube and the Rhine.

Epidorix stood nearby as well, anxious to put to the test his new-found skills of battle.

Venutius had fully split from Cartimandua, their joint politics a melding of the past. Those who had felt the fairness of his just decisions, meted out with the diligence of communal thought, those who had felt the force of an unruly Roman backlash, insistent on quarters and supplies, and those conscripted into a Roman army, forced to raise the swords of their Celtic ancestors in battle that never was theirs, felt compelled to join the warrior band. For Epidorix, a chance to demonstrate his manhood alongside an older brother he had long admired but rarely seen, and a chance to raise the sword of his Celtic Iberian ancestors, laid to rest for several generations, proved reason enough to enter the hasty fray.

Cartimandua, mindful of the rebellion, had organized her warriors with permission from Rome. Certain she could win, the strength of the Brigantes tribe and the fortress of the palace city behind her, she threw very few of her armaments into preparation for battle, despite the pleadings of her seasoned warriors and advisors, preferring to save them for the battles enlisted by Rome.

Cartimandua's warriors moved to the south, hoping to quell the rebellion before it reached the palace city, disrupting the wealth she had built on an acquiescence to Rome. Venutius, with an equal band of warriors, met them on the vast plains of the tribal countryside, his greatest defense the wrath of a righteous rabble.

Though it had been long since Venutius had engaged in battle of any kind, he was surrounded by seasoned warriors. Segovax, a noble who, though surrounded by tenant farmers willing to defend the land, had always led them in battle, driving off the raiders of the south. Carvilius, who had deserted Cartimandua's warriors to fight alongside the prince consort whose judicial skill and politics he admired. And Lugotorix, an ancient warrior and artisan whose side Venutius had once taken in a dispute in which Cartimandua had tried to cede the lands meted out to him as payment for years of devoted service.

Venutius called council as soon as news of the approaching forces reached them. Sending the messenger to refresh himself with the bread they had baked along the way from gifts of grain, and cheeses from farmers sympathetic to their cause, he gathered his advisors informally about him in a clearing now rife with the daisies of spring.

Segovax, used to meeting the enemy head on, favored that tactic in facing Cartimandua's warriors. Carvilius, a warrior in his prime, who had shown great bravery upon the battlefield, favored that tactic as well. Epidorix, brought into council by Venutius to learn the ways of the island Celts, anxious to learn the skills he had practiced so long in secret, agreed. It was only Lugotorix who saw difficulty with that plan.

"Cartimandua's warriors are skilled in battle and have more experience than our farmers and artisans," he said, as he squatted his solid frame among the grasses, carefully musing on the enemy's strengths. Segovax, seated next to him, cross-legged in the grasses just now turning green with the mists of spring, listened silently, nodding in deference to his superior knowledge.

"Though their numbers are not great, and their armaments few," Lugotorix continued, "our armaments are fewer." He paused, then continued. "We have few chariots to pull away our wounded or cause a stir among the enemy."

Carvilius spoke. "Cartimandua's warriors are not anxious to meet their tribal neighbors on the field of battle, especially in a cause brought on only by royal edict. They will not be in a hurry to bring full honor to the gods."

"Our warriors," said Venutius "await with the spirit of their ancestors. Many would have preferred to keep their lands and taxes from Rome."

Lugotorix spoke once again. "We must keep our strengths hidden from our enemy until the time is ripe to send them at once upon the battlefield. We will lay in wait in the forests north. When the enemy approaches, we will keep our best warriors hidden, while our greatest numbers attack upon the plains."

In the end, the others agreed to Lugotorix's plan, adding expertise in areas in which they were familiar, and assigning tasks according to individual skills. Cavilius, familiar with the enemy's tactical thought, would lead the first attack. Segovax, a superb horseman, would lead their best warriors from the forest to the battle. Lugotorix, covered with scars of battle but more feeble than the rest, would remain in hiding to direct the cause of battle.

As they broke their council, Venutius directed Epidorix to alert their warriors to their plans of battle. The youth complied, anxious to take on new found responsibility, returning as the sun went down. Then, the brothers ate a simple meal beneath the stars. As they ate, Epidorix shared his news from home.

"Father grows weary collecting the heavy taxes the Romans levy upon his neighbors," he said, as he laid a slab of cheese upon some bread, drinking water dipped from a nearby stream from a skin held cool laid into a saddle bag. "Mother tries to keep his spirits up, sending him to the baths daily, devoting herself to keeping the Roman customs, and dedicated to the Roman dress. But, I know she secretly yearns for the costumes of the past." He paused to lift a morsel of fish they had roasted over the campfire, then continued. "Often, I see her lift her grandmother's tunics, gay with the embroidery of the woodland, from the plain oak chest she keeps in a corner of her bed chamber, when she thinks no one will spy her."

"We must lift the Roman oppression," he said.

"We must overturn Cartimandua's command," Venutius returned. "Only then will we be able to lead the Brigantes tribe to reclaim what was rightfully theirs. The right to lift the swords of their ancestors in their own defense, the right to plow their fields and harvest their grain to lay upon their own tables."

As they finished their meal, they pulled their blankets from their saddle bags, settling under the stars to slumber, each with his own thoughts of the conflict ahead.

On the morrow, Venutius arose with the first rays of the morning sun. Epidorix, already bathed in a nearby stream, was painting his body with the blue dye of the woad plant. The brothers greeted each other, holding a silent embrace, long denied them with seasons of separation. As they parted, a messenger arrived with word for Venutius of Cartimandua's warriors, expected to reach them as the sun shone directly over the plains where they were camped.

As they waited, Epidorix once again practiced his sword play, running through or putting to flight many an imagined warrior. As the enemy arrived, Cavilius led the greatest numbers of their band to meet them upon the plain. Venutius, without benefit of mount, entered the fray, downing quickly a number of palace warriors. As the strength of the enemy waned, Segovax led out the hidden warriors on mount, setting the remaining enemy to flee the plain for the safety of the palace gates.

As the cheer of victory rose from the lips of a battle-weary lot, Venutius looked round for Epidorix. But, the youth lay among the daisies of the field, his last breath drawn in combat with an enemy warrior more skilled than he, a smile upon his face. Venutius held him as he sobbed.

Then, leading his band north, Venutius cut down the enemy forces, his rebel band gaining the strength of victory. But, as they neared the walls of the palace city, the gates opened to pour forth a host of Roman troops, called for by Cartimandua to quell the rebellion her own warriors had been unable to subdue.

The strength of sheer numbers brought a quick defeat, forcing Venutius into the asylum of a neighboring tribe not yet bowed to the Roman enemy. As his mount made tracks for the west, he left behind forever a tribe in which he had spent his reign as prince consort keeping the mantle of peace.

Chapter Eighteen

Prasutagus lay amid the bedcovers of the softest skins that palace huntsmen were able to bring down upon Iceni lands. Alaina and Valeda stood beside him. Astrinellia, not far in a massive chair of oak, its back carved with the playful goddesses of the woodlands, worked her fingers over a pale, blue stretch of linen, dyed with the hyacinths of spring, turning the length of an embroidery stitch into the pale, pink of a wild rosebud.

Boudicca, weary from days of attending her very ill husband, sat nearby upon a wooden stool, her simple, deep green tunic, edged with squares of golden thread, barely brushing the hard, clay floor, her long, red tresses pulled back and held by a single strand of braided deep green linen.

Prasutagus, weak from the illness that had assailed him last Beltane, lay nearly prone upon the bed, his slender frame more slender, his long, white locks, now grown thin and wispy, his features sharp upon a wan and pale countenance.

Several times he had tried to draw Boudicca into talk of affairs of state, only to fall into a fitful slumber.

Mandarus, Prasutagus' long-time trusted aide, had been called into full-time service as temporary regent to the Iceni tribe, conferring as often as possible with its king, gravely ill, still insistent in his role as peacemaker and client-king of Rome.

Though Boudicca had long silently disagreed with Prasutagus' stand on the Roman government, she had never risen up against him, at his side as he asked his tribesmen to lay down their arms in their own defense, to lift them only as Rome's needs arose, conquering tribe after tribe on their tiny island.

Beltanes and Sanheims came and went, marked only in the minds of the Iceni Celts, no longer a ritual in the lush woodlands of Iceni forests, the Druids long driven out to seek refuge on the Isle of Mona.

Boudicca thought often of Diviticus and the lessons he had taught, the council he had given, and tales he had shared of tribal and inter-tribal mediations. She thought often, also, of the rites of Beltane, the garlands she had strung from the newly risen violets and anemones of the woodland floor, flung about a newly-carved image of Sequanna, a plea for a lush harvest that almost always came. She thought of the sacred white hare, once roaming free through the Iceni woodlands, now brought down to grace the Roman soldier's table. Of Sanheim, of tales told to Mandorix long after they both should have been aslumber, and their shutters flung open ready to greet the rays of dawn.

In turn, Prasutagus was allowed to reign unencumbered and the privilege of continuing to mint coins. His power and tribal respect remained intact, accompanied by a watchfulness from Rome. Despite increasingly heavy tax burdens, the Iceni tribe continued to prosper, its crops bounty for the Roman tables, its artisans, once crafting the helmets, chariots and swords of Celtic battle, the massive oak chairs of the royal palace, turned to crafting weapons for the Roman army, a temple to honor Claudius in the nearby city of Camulodunum built for the isle's battle-weary Roman soldiers, and tables and chairs for Roman villas.

As Prasutagus stirred, he called for water, bringing Boudicca to his side to pour the precious liquid from a golden urn, complete with woodland stag chasing a woodland boar about its middle, into a beautiful silver goblet, the Iceni crest emblazoned upon its side.

Boudicca had long stopped tempting him with his favorite meats, trying only bits of bread and cheese, which Prasutagus most often refused. As she held the goblet to his lips, lifting his head, now barely heavy to her grasp, to drink, she fixed his bedcovers as best she could about him, for despite that the warmth of summer was upon them, Prasutagus suffered from cold.

As she lifted him slightly and leaned him against the heavier skins, so that he could view the brilliant yellow of the Iris, the pale purple of the foxglove, and starkest white of the summer daisies of the courtyard, attended now by the thrush and the wren, whose songs flowed brightly through the open shutters, he spoke softly.

"Boudicca," he said, gasping for the breath now denied him, "we must talk of affairs of state." He lay back upon the softest doeskins behind him.

"Yes, Prasutagus," she answered, as she lay the goblet back upon its table. "You speak, and I shall listen." She pulled a stool close to sit, leaning her ear very near his withered lips.

"Boudicca," he said slowly, "Mandarus will guide you in state affairs. Our coffers are full and we still prosper, thanks to the beneficence of Rome." He paused, gathering his breath once again to continue. "To further our connection, and to press for further allowances from Rome, I have left half our riches to Alaina and Valeda, and half to the Emperor Claudius of Rome. Thus, Claudius should not resent you, allowing you to be queen of Iceni in peace as I have been king." As he finished, spent from his labors, he fell back once again upon the piled doeskins.

"No, my king," she answered, "we must get you well." She mopped his brow, heavy with beads of sweat, with a soft linen rinsed in a basin of cool water pulled from the stream along the courtyard garden.

"Boudicca," he said, "my time has come to pass over to the Other World. I am ready." He paused, gathering breath once again. "I shall see my father, his helmet atop his head, bearing the gods of Iceni battle, astride his favorite mount. My mother will be sitting, as always, perched upon a low oaken stool, waiting, gently pulling a needle of ram's horn through a piece of silk or linen."

He paused, then continued. "Boudicca, you have been to me a good wife and faithful queen. Our daughters grow into lovely maidens. Soon, without the help of the holy days, or the rites of spring or autumn, they will be ready for a match. Mandarus will help you make a good one, for the blood of the Iceni flow within them." Then, as the spirit ebbed within him, he lay back, falling into a gentle slumber.

As Boudicca turned, she spied Alaina and Valeda, huddled together upon an oaken bench, their tears of grief dropping gently upon their golden tresses flowing free about their shoulders, the hue of the locks of Prasutagus' youth. The rays of the noonday sun glistened in upon them.

"My daughters," she said, as she hurried to embrace them, "you must ride out upon the countryside. You have been by your father's side and a comfort to him, but now you must rest. He slumbers now in peace."

She lifted them from the bench as she continued. "Your favorite mounts await, for they too need to run free across the hillsides and the plains. I will see that the kitchen servants pack you a tidy noonday meal."

As they walked slowly toward the doorway, Astrinellia arose, striding toward them to put her arms about them as they headed for the pantry larder.

Boudicca, pulling her stool close to Prasutagus' bedside, sat, admiring the yellow of the daisies, the soft brown of a woodland fawn of Astrinellia's embroidery which lay nearby, patting Prasutagus' hand as he occasionally woke.

Grooms brushed and oiled the coats of mounts, laying oats and hay in stalls for feed, and leading the mares in foal, the stallions eager to run the plains, gently out among the grasses to exercise, as Alaina and Valeda entered the palace stables. Vibillius, Alaina's friend since childhood, brought the young princess to Nerthus' stall, a carrot in hand to feed the ailing pony. Alaina entered the stall, gently patting Nerthus' white coat, the pony laying upon his side.

As he recognized Alaina, raising a soft, low whinny of welcome, he licked slowly the carrot that she held. Nerthus had been a pet as well as mount, and he and Alaina had ridden the forests and plains together, watching carefully the path of the sacred white hare, Nerthus eating his oats, Alaina her noonday meal upon a linen cloth, as they rested in a shady woodland glade. Now, Nerthus was unable to leave his stall, the feebleness of old age upon him, but Vibillius gently helped him to eat, giving him sweet treats from the palace larder. Alaina visited him often.

Vibillius helped Alaina and Valeda choose a mount. Though the princesses preferred the bare back of the chestnut roans they had chosen, they gave in to Vibillius' plea for a proper saddle, refusing all help to mount.

As they went for a run across the plains, their pale, blond locks flying in the noonday breeze, the city gates farther and farther behind them, they slowed to a gallop, then a trot, the rays of the sun warming their backs through their lightweight tunics as they rode.

It had been seventeen summers since Alaina had entered the Iceni palace as a newborn, fifteen for Valeda. Now, slowed to a trot, Alaina sat erect upon her roan, her poise a likeness of a youthful Prasutagus riding into battle, her slender frame draped with an unadorned saffron tunic, her only jewelry a golden torque about her neck. Her delicate features belied her forthright nature, her bubbling laugh heard often about the palace hallways.

Valeda, though similar in frame and features, was a contrast to her sister, in past sitting quietly in a corner musing upon a childhood toy, now moving quickly through the palace hallways as she learned her royal duties at the elbow of a patient Mandarus.

Neither chatted now as they rode, their grief eclipsing their thoughts. As they neared a forest, the huge sycamores and hawthorns abloom with summer foliage, they spotted a clearing not far into the woodland. "A good place to take our noonday meal," said Alaina, as she spied an old oak to tie her roan, tethering Valeda's beside it. A stream ran nearby, letting their mounts drink from the cool waters.

Valeda unpacked their meal, laying it upon a linen of many hues that Astrinellia had added to the saddle pack. The creamy goat cheese, the freshly baked bread, the honey gathered from the palace hives, were enhanced by a gentle, summer breeze. They left the linen only to drink the cool waters of the stream.

"What will we do when Papa claims his place in the Other World?" asked Valeda.

"Mama is queen. She will lead the Iceni tribe as Papa did before her," answered Alaina. "But," she added, "she will be too busy for our usual woodland jaunts. I heard Papa say the Romans increase their demands as they topple our island's tribes. Only the small tribes escape, like the Catuvellauni who gave haven to Venutius." She sighed, the memories of Venutius and his visits upon her.

"We must help Mama," she continued, "and take more chores upon ourselves, for she will not ask us."

Valeda was silent, as her duty lay before her. "Mandarus says he will find a match for us both," she said. She paused, then continued. "You are first, because you are older."

Alaina giggled, the first hint of laughter upon her face since Prasutagus' illness. "I wonder who he will choose," she said, "for there is no one of noble birth within our city gates." She stopped, musing upon a nearby hawthorn, its leafy branches home to a woodland thrush's nest, an ebon butterfly, crossed with white and scarlet, flitting about it. "I wish it could be Valerin," she continued. "For though he is shy, and looks away when I fix my gaze upon him, he is strong, helping me to my saddle with the strength of seven warriors. But," she added, "he is only a stable groom."

"Mama says Mandarus must choose from a tribe already aligned with the Roman state," said Valeda. "It is Papa's wish."

"Well, it will be many Beltanes before the rites of joining," answered Alaina, her head cocked to catch the rays of the early afternoon sun peering through the densely foliaged woodland, her voice suddenly filled with the laughter she had known since birth. "I have many seasons to ride the Iceni plains," she continued. "To walk the palace halls, to listen to the handmaidens gossip, to visit the carefully swept huts of Iceni farmers when Mama will let me, to rock their babies and bring them treats of honey, to watch them milk their goats or plow, as Mama promised Linnea she would."

As she spoke, she rose from the linen throw to follow the path that wound along the crooked stream. Valeda jumped up to follow. It was often in their afternoon jaunts they meandered about the woodlands, checking to spot the new fawns, the baby brown hares, and the baby thrush, all born in the spring. If they were lucky, and very quiet, they might see a wren or sparrow in awkward first flight.

They walked along the woodland, eyeing the moon daisies, the pale purple geranium, and the purple and yellow vetch of the clearing beyond. As the sun began to set, they made their way back to their tethered mounts, gathered up their linen and the remains of their meal into their saddle pack, untethered their mounts, riding through the woodland paths and across the plains, the grasses now filled with the bluebells, poppies and foxgloves of summer, toward the city gates.

When they arrived, hastening to Prasutagus' bedchamber, they took their place next to Astrinellia, her embroidery set aside, her hands clasping Prasutagus'. Boudicca, her tunic now creased from wear and carefully folded about her, dozing in the corner in a massive, oaken chair.

The lifeless body of Prasutagus lay in state upon an iron cart emblazoned with an Iceni crest, drawn by horses all veterans of Celtic battle. His scarlet tunic, placed over a pair of indigo trousers, covered by a deerskin robe, bore the Iceni crest as well. A golden torque, crafted with the Iceni gods of battle lay about his neck. His helmet, iron with embedded gold and coral, a bronze eagle atop it, lay nearby. His sword, sheathed on a scabbard of bronze scrolled with silver and gold, lay nearby as well. His large, oval shield lay beside him.

His passing had been a quiet one, a last gasp for breath during a fitful slumber. Now, his soul had slipped to the Other World.

Crowds drawn from Iceni lands had gathered at the palace grounds to bury him, a king to whom allegiance had been easy. His courage in battle had never failed, his concern for the well-being of his tribe a constant, their prosperity evident in their dress, their mounts, their homes, the commerce of the tribe.

Despite the restrictions of Rome, and the absence of Druids, Prasutagus was being given a Celtic funeral, a wish he had voiced before his death. Iceni tribesmen who remembered the funeral rites, aided by Mandarus who represented continued affairs of state, were there to perform them.

Boudicca looked stately, drawn in an open carriage which followed Prasutagus' cart. Her tunic, the hue of the skies on a sunny day, was fastened with a golden brooch depicting two nightingales in song, her arms adorned with a pair of golden bracelets, her fingers bearing rings of Iceni crests. Her lightweight mantle, the hue of the pale primrose, was woven with golden threads. Her long red tresses, wound about her head, were dressed in the traditional Celtic manner.

Her daughters stood beside her, a symbol of Iceni dynasty, their tears of grief now dried, their bearing a credit to regal dignity. Their long, blond tresses, no longer running free about their shoulders, thickened with lime and wound about their heads, had been dressed by Boudicca's own handmaidens, the long coils held by clasps of silver and gold. Iceni crests of golden thread edged the indigo of their tunics.

Boudicca stood silent, a symbol of the continuity she hoped to achieve for Prasutagus' sake. Alaina and Valeda, quieted by the solemnity of the occasion, chatted softly, pointing out friends, children of nobles and artisans once called often to the palace for council, now less frequently since Rome had overrun their isle.

Prasutagus was to be buried on palace grounds, a tradition of Iceni kings. A spot beneath a favorite chestnut tree had been chosen by Mandarus and his council, and Boudicca and Astrinellia had agreed.

As they arrived, the grounds beneath the tree already prepared, they stepped down from the carriage, taking their place among Mandarus and his sages. Astrinellia arrived soon after. Olovicus, an elder tribesman, once a student of the Druids, began. "We are here to aid Prasutagus in a safe journey to the Other World. We bear gifts, so that he should not want, and we add to the joy of the Other World." He stopped, nodding to a young helper, a palace messenger chosen for the zeal he gave to his duties, and to represent Prasutagus' devotion to his tribe's affairs of state. The youth, not much older than Alaina, stepped forward, his deerskin tunic embroidered with the Iceni crest and arranged in a formal manner, a wooden cage bearing a pair of doves clasped tightly in his hands.

Olovicus continued. "Let us add to the peace of the Other World," he said. As he spoke, the young messenger lifted the door of the cage, setting free the doves. The doves, fluttering slightly, then gaining their bearings, flew directly toward the sun.

The sage spoke again. "Let us also add to the joy of song in the Other World," he said. At that, another palace youth, a minstrel-in-training, let loose a nightingale.

He continued, waving his arms as he continued the ancient rite. "Now, we can add to its sustenance and beauty. Queen Boudicca, you may lay upon the earth your offerings."

Boudicca stepped forward, her handmaidens laden with Prasutagus' favorite cheese, bits of honey, a freshly baked bread pulled earlier from the palace ovens, and garlands of rose petals. She reached over to lay the offerings upon the earth herself.

Alaina and Valeda followed, placing upon Prasutagus' tomb the shiny stones they had gathered on their woodland jaunts, bowls of silver and gold, and pieces of coral they had smoothed to a fine finish themselves. Astrinellia added Prasutagus' favorite flagon, and a carving of Duana, a goddess of the hunt he had crafted for her as a child.

Then, Olovicus continued. "We wish Prasutagus a safe journey, where he will dwell in peace, among trees with crystal leaves which shine forever in the never-ending sun, and forever hear the song of the birds." He lowered his arms, giving the sign which ended the rite.

Boudicca climbed back into the carriage, along with Mandarus, who sought to give their tribesmen a visible sign of continuity. Alaina and Valeda rode along as well.

Boudicca gave orders to the palace servants to set out the bread, the cheese and the honey they had prepared, and to begin turning the spits set earlier over the open pits and laden with the boar and game brought down by the palace huntsmen. As they rode toward the palace gates, Boudicca knew that what she had studied for, early as a child at Diviticus' knee, lay ahead.

Chapter Nineteen

It had been nearly a fortnight since Prasutagus had been laid beneath the chestnut tree. The crowds had dispersed, making their way back to their homes along the winding city streets or the fields of Iceni lands.

The palace had returned to normal. Mandarus sat in the great hall, his council at table nearby. Boudicca remained at his side, helping to mediate disputes, checking with artisans on designing and minting coins, and placating tribesmen on taxes newly levied to support the Roman army.

Astrinellia, still in mourning for the brother she adored, spent her days arranging flowers, embroidering pillow and footstool covers, and the edgings of special tunics for Alaina and Valeda. The two princesses, true to their word, gave support to Boudicca by paying attention to their studies of affairs of state, and by making certain she relaxed on walks along the carefully manicured paths of the palace gardens, spying the new phlox and daylilies of late summer, and listening to the minstrels, the shutters flung open to let in the summer breeze, by moonlight.

As morn came with the rain upon the shutters of her bedchamber, Boudicca arose, bathing to chase away the scent of the murky fog drifting through the cracks of her bedchamber windows, and the dreariness of another rainy day. As her handmaidens added the lovely scent of lavender to the heated waters of her bath, she lavished in the aroma, leaning back, her head upon the edge of the iron tub, its feet the shape of an eagle's claw. Her handmaidens added soaps the scent of woodland flowers, shaped like the stags and hares of the forest.

As she rubbed these upon her body, her arms still soft and tender, her hands roughened from years of reigning in her mounts along the hills and the plains of the Iceni, she thought of Caractacus, his detention in Rome, the nine years he had stood against the Romans, the rebellion of the Silures to defend their chieftain, and their defeat. She thought of Venutius, known to the Romans as fierce in battle, but without a tribe to lead, living alone among the Catuvellauni, a small tribe which because of its size had escaped the wrath of the Romans.

Boudicca arose from the bath, rubbing her arms with the perfumed oils her handmaidens had made ready, and donning a proper tunic, a deep indigo linen edged only with golden Iceni crests. Her tresses she had dressed in the traditional Celtic manner.

As she walked the halls of the palace, she thought of the tasks and decisions to be made. Rome pressed further with demands, increasing taxes and demanding more and more goods. The neighboring colony of Camulodunum, set up by the Romans to house their veterans of battle, increased demands as well, asking for tribesmen to attend to the great temple of Claudius, which the Iceni had built on request from Rome, to repair its many Roman columns, to keep it from the earthly elements which eroded its stately facade. With more veterans daily filling the city, all idle and often drunk with ale, the demands increased, the lawlessness as well.

Boudicca entered the great hall and took her place beside Mandarus in a large, oaken chair elaborately carved with the larger animals of the hunt. "Who will come before us this morn," she asked, as she seated herself more securely in the chair.

"First," he said, "we will hear from the artisans who will fashion our newest coin, its design dictated in part by Rome. One side must carry a raised image of the temple built to worship Claudius, the other a raised image of his head. Marius and Dartius, our most experienced artisans of coin, will appear before us, their etchings already complete upon the softest shale. We must approve the drawings, the head must be befitting an emperor of Rome, the temple must appear divine, so not to offend the Romans."

"We must also," he said, "find a way to appease our farmers and our artisans. Rome demands more food and the urns, the ewers, the anklets and golden arm decorations set with our coral, more and more prized by Roman women."

"In turn," he added, "we continue to mint coins and are allowed to buy goods from the Continent. But, our artisans are overworked and our farmers work harder with less food upon their own tables."

As he spoke, a messenger arrived, sent by Venutius, his journey from the Catuvellauni lands evident by the dust still covering his mantle. "I bear a message for Queen Boudicca," he said, as he regained his breath and his composure. "It is from Prince Venutius."

"Please tell me it at once,' she answered, leaning forward to better hear the messenger.

"Prince Venutius says he would be with you now in your loss to aid you, but for the danger of leaving the safety of the Catuvellauni, whose loose alliance with Rome leaves them neither a city-state or a province of Rome. 'I know you will do a good job and honor the memory of Prasutagus. You are very fit to be Queen. I think often of you, of Alaina and Valeda, of our many woodland jaunts along the Iceni and Coritani lands. May Sequanna and all the Celtic gods be with you, and may you wear the mistletoe of worship in your thoughts'."

As she mused upon the message, in her memory the first mistletoe Venutius as a youth had climbed an oak to fetch, she bade the messenger take palace hospitality, Then, Dartius and Marius took their place before her.

Marius spoke. "We bring drawings of both Claudius and his temple. We also believe we may mint this coin larger than others before. A token of homage to both the emperor and his worship."

Boudicca took the proposed drawings from Marius, thanking both artisans for their devoted efforts. As she studied them, a city gate guard burst forth into the great hall without announcement, his disheveled arrival a signal to halt proceedings. He hastened directly to Boudicca.

"Queen Boudicca," he said, trying desperately to catch his breath, "the veterans of Camulodunum have broken through our city gates. With no ready defense, we are helpless. They have felled our guards. They ride directly for the palace."

At that, the din of a noisy rabble reached the palace. In one sudden moment, without arms at the ready, Boudicca felt the doom of an entire tribe.

The veterans of Camulodunum, drunk with power and ale, reached the palace gates quickly breaking through and quelling the little resistance the guards were able to muster. Breaking through the palace doors was easy, the heavy wood of the oaken doors and the bars which were quickly secured by the palace guard quickly falling to the enemy ax.

The Romans swarmed through, routing out servants and royal family alike, in a frenzy to subjugate the city. Servants were chained together, Astrinellia and Mandarus with them. Boudicca was kept aside.

Nowhere did Boudicca see Alaina or Valeda. Unable to catch a servant's eye, or speak directly to one, she was left without word of either of her daughters. The terror increased as well as the screams of routed servants, unable to hide behind the great oaken chests or iron tubs, behind a pile of skins, from the plunder of Roman soldiers.

Boudicca stood alone in the great hall, surrounded by the group of veterans assigned to guard her. Her demands to know their intentions and to point out that Iceni lands were protected by Roman pact were met by the icy stares and menacing gestures of her captors.

As she stood, she was forced to view the exodus of every palace servant, those who were new and those who had given years of loyal and devoted service to Prasutagus and his family. Astrinellia, her terror overtaking her normally delicate countenance, limped along, keeping up as best she could.

The long line, palace servants now chained together with Astrinellia, Mandarus, and the palace council, were forced single file through the now open doorways, obviously bound for the galley of a Roman slave ship. Boudicca stilled as she saw the back of Astrinellia, shoved forward by a drunken Roman soldier.

Uncertain of her own fate, Boudicca waited, silent, her captors occupied with thoughts of swelling the ranks of slaves and plunder. Her thoughts turned to Alaina and Valeda, her hopes that they were safely hidden.

As she thought, Marcus Quintillius, now leader of the veterans, arrived, charging directly into the great hall, shouting orders as he went. "Check every Iceni household, lest it harbor weapons. Take, also, what we need to replenish our dwindling grain and our supplies. Order every Iceni tribesman housed near the palace to journey to palace grounds by sundown."

At that, he turned toward Boudicca, sneering as he spoke. "You Celts think you can let a woman rule a kingdom. Your husband, because of the devotion of the Iceni tribe, was useful to Rome, bringing himself and the empire great wealth, forging the weapons of battle, sending warriors to aid the Roman cause."

He continued. "But we, the veterans of long years of battle upon this island tire of Claudius' pacts. We demand the subjugation of this isle as we were promised."

He turned, motioning the guards to surround her, blocking her escape and barring all news of Alaina and Valeda. "Hold her here until sundown," he ordered, making his way from the great hall.

As Boudicca peered through the open shutters, the sun sank slowly, making way for the light of the moon. As she watched, the noise of the crowd, shuffling slowly up the hillside, reached her ears.

The sunset brought the return of Marcus Quintillius, tall upon his mount. He dismounted, turning toward the great hall, long strides carrying him toward it. As he entered, he motioned his men to take Boudicca out into the courtyard, now bright with the light of torches. They prodded her as she walked.

The veterans took their place among the crowd, their gloved hands upon their swords. Marcus Quintillius raised his arm for silence, then spoke. "The Romans shall rule," he shouted, his voice carrying into the silence of the crisp night, the stars bright in a clear, dark sky.

He stopped, turning his head toward Boudicca's guards. "Lash her to that tree," he ordered, pointing to the largest oak in the courtyard. As the guards obeyed, he continued. "We show you that your queen has no power. We, the Romans, now reign over the Iceni tribe."

He stopped, then continued. "You must follow our demands. To build more temples for the worship of the divine Claudius, to turn more grain into bread for the Roman tables, to halt the minting of coins. The goods of the Continent are now forbidden to you."

As he spoke, a guard appeared behind Boudicca, bearing the length of a very large whip. At Quintillius' signal, he raised the whip, his aim the back of the lashed Boudicca. As the long lash whipped against her back, her anger, suppressed during the reign of Prasutagus, rose within her. Visions of the Coritani woodlands where she, Caractacus and Venutius once ran free, the Iceni plains, where Alaina and Valeda took their jaunts, all passed about her.

But, the sting of the lash brought reminders of earthly pain. Each strike brought tears of pain, and finally cries of agony. As it ended, Boudicca fell nearly lifeless against the tree.

Marcus Quintillius cut her down himself, standing over her body, still upon the mist of the ground. "We Romans are victors," he shouted. "Now, go back to your homes. Toil for Claudius and the Roman empire."

As he spoke, he climbed his mount, ready to lead the veterans back to Camulodunum. As the clatter of their horses' hooves became once again a distant din, Boudicca stirred.

As she made her way down the palace hallways, frantic to find Alaina and Valeda, unmindful of her wounds as she went, Boudicca's countenance changed. Long an aid to Prasutagus' stance on Rome, to save the Iceni from battle, to preserve their wealth, she had secretly admired Caractacus' stand against the Roman army, the Silures' continued battle despite the confinement of their king to Rome.

She thought of her duty to the Iceni, how she must rebuild the palace, how she must remind Claudius of the Roman-Iceni pact, with hopes that he would honor it. Dartius and Marius had remained behind to help with matters of state, Dartius' wife Marinna to scour the countryside for palace servants. She thought, also, of Astrinellia, soft and gentle, forced into a life of Roman slavery.

As she reached the kitchen, past the ransacked larder, the remnants of its grain strewn about the hallway, she spied the full destruction the Romans had brought upon the Iceni royal family. Alaina and Valeda lay upon the clay of the floor, in pools of their own blood mixed with the semen of Roman soldiers, their tunics torn from their bodies, their feeble moans the only sign of life.

She bent down to soothe them as best she could, stroking their tresses now matted with blood. As she knelt, she pondered the dawn through the broken shutters now breaking over the empty courtyard.

Chapter Twenty

Boudicca stood at the rear of a wicker wood chariot, her tresses wound up under a newly-forged bronze and iron helmet, studded with coral, silver and gold. Her bright green woolen mantle covered a simple earthen-hued tunic, a large, golden torque emblazoned with the Iceni crest about her neck. A bronze shield sculpted with the Iceni gods and the stags and the hares of the woodlands and a javelin lay beside her, a leather-sheathed dagger about her waist.

Alaina and Valeda stood at the helm, driving the chariot bent for Camulodunum, pulled by two chestnut and ebony ponies bred for battle, their harnesses adorned with carefully crafted enameled bits edged with gold and silver, their manes with brightly hued plumes. The men of the Iceni tribe followed, those who had trained as warriors before Rome had invaded the Briton island, and those who had left their fields and their plows, their forges and kilns, to train as well.

The Trinobantes had joined them, bringing up the rear, their chief Ortevegas at their lead. It had been easy for Boudicca to persuade Ortevegas to combine their forces in an attack on

Camulodunum. Conquered by the Romans, but long neglected by them, the Trinobantes longed for their freedom.

Despite the healing of the welts upon her back raised by the Roman lash, Boudicca had trained for battle, enlisting the aid of the best Iceni warriors brought to the palace to live. Alaina and Valeda had regained their strength and most of their spirit, nursed tenderly by the Iceni women, though memories of violence and the loss of Astrinellia still touched them.

The late autumn had brought a golden yellow to the chestnut and poplar trees, and except for a few corn daisies and hawkweed, the wild flowers had disappeared from the hills and plains they rode through. The fruit of the chestnut hung low and the red of the elm stood brilliant in the sun.

Boudicca had planned the attack on Camulodunum along with Indomarius, the oldest of the Iceni warriors. Decorated with the scars of many battles, he sat in council with the Iceni queen, Ortevegas, and a group of warriors from the Iceni and Trinobantes tribes.

The Iceni were easy for Boudicca to convince as well. Long loyal to the beloved Prasutagus, the diplomacy he practiced and the pact he had forged no longer honored by the Romans, outraged at the attack upon their queen and the royal household, they longed for the revenge of a Celtic warrior, no longer a Roman pawn.

Indomarius had insisted upon a surprise attack, keeping the day a secret among the council, rallying the tribes on the very day of attack, a plan to enter the city on their mounts, leveling buildings as they went, then meet the enemy in battle upon the ground.

As they rode, Indomarius pulled his mount alongside the chariot, matching his stallion's pace to the ponies'. "We near the city," he shouted to Boudicca. "The woodland and hills we now pass lie only paces from Camulodunum."

"I shall alert Alaina and Valeda to add speed," she answered, "lest the Romans be alerted by our dust."

Indomarius then turned to return to his place alongside Ortevegas. As he went, he shouted, "May the gods of the ancients and the gods of the Iceni battle be with you."

Boudicca raised her arm in salute, then turned toward Alaina and Valeda. "We must drive the ponies faster," she shouted. "We are nearly upon Camulodunum."

"We have arrived," shouted Alaina. "The city rises before us."

At that, Boudicca gave the signal to charge, the large horde of warriors falling in behind the wicker wood chariot. The city lay before them, unprotected by guards or gate, stone ramparts or the wood of a stockade fence.

They rode with a frenzy known only to the long repressed, hacking at buildings, taking a torch to those unyielding to the ax. Roman soldiers, caught in the sloth of their own gambling and ale, scattered everywhere, unarmed, seeking refuge in the great, stone temple built for the worship of Claudius, raised at the edge of the city. A statue of Victory, built upon a pedestal in the city square, fell forward, its shattered wings and outstretched arms victim of the rumble.

The fires of Iceni and Trinobantes torches blazed behind them, the planks and rubble of wooden housing strewn about. As they rode, Boudicca gave the signal to ride toward the temple, calling Indomarius and Ortevegas to surround the great, stone structure, its columns supporting a massive, stone image of Claudius, its entrance guarded by two large stone lions.

As the Iceni and Trinobantes assembled, greater in number than the residents of Camulodunum, Boudicca called to Alaina to pull the chariot alongside Indomarius. As the two tribes closed ranks, flank to flank, facing the temple, she spoke. "We have leveled every building," she said, facing the elder warrior, "save the temple. In their haste, the Romans have taken no food to stave their hunger within the walls which now hold them captive. We shall wait till hunger drives them forth upon this grassy plain."

"We shall be able to withstand," he said. "Our saddle packs hold provisions, and we have gathered the great stores of meat and bread taken liberally from the Iceni and the Trinobantes to feed a Roman army that tills no field nor knows the art of the hunt."

He paused, moving his weary frame about in the saddle. "In their haste," he said, "the Romans gathered their weapons and their armor. But, as they pour forth, they will not be able to assemble in advance as the Roman army is trained. They must enter battle as we do, warrior to warrior, sword to sword. We shall fight them on horseback and on this grassy plain, driving them to the river behind us."

At that, Indomarius took his leave, returning to help Ortevegas close ranks around the temple. Boudicca turned to Alaina and Valeda. "We must make camp along the river," she said, "so we will be at our full strength on the morrow when the sun rises in the morn. The Trinobantes will keep watch until evening and the Iceni when the moon shows in the sky."

As Boudicca spoke, Alaina signaled the chariot's ponies, standing firm with their plumes of battle still mostly intact, pulling gently on their reins to head them toward the river which flowed along the hillside below the city of Camulodunum, now ashes and rubble, the only monument to the battle-weary Roman veterans it had housed.

The ponies trotted the hillside, its grasses the brown of autumn, the river flowed gently beneath the pinks and violets of the sunset. As they reached the water, Boudicca pointed to a stand of beech trees, their golden-red leaves ideal for shelter beneath the darkening sky. Valeda pulled loose the heavy woolen blankets lashed to the chariot's sides, Alaina released the ponies, tying them to a tree towering over the river's edge, its roots wet with the waters of the evening tide, its trunk slightly bent from the force of the wind whipping it as a sapling. She patted them gently as they drank.

As Valeda spread the blankets along the ground among the beech trees, Boudicca pulled from the chariot a pouch of salted meats, a pack of cheeses, some bread freshly baked with the ground wheat of the palace larder, and an empty flask which she filled with the cooled, evening waters of the river. As the three sat, Boudicca spoke. "We will drive the Romans from our shores," she said. "But, the cost may be great."

She paused, looking toward the river. "The Silures fight on," she continued, "but without their king to lead them, they neither win nor lose. And, Venutius avoids the capture of the Brigantes in the shelter of the Catuvellauni, but he no longer lifts a sword in defense of a Celtic tribe."

She turned her gaze back toward her daughters. "I am strong once again, Sequanna protects me, and the Iceni warriors are determined to repel the Roman army," she said. "But, should I be felled by a Roman sword, we must make plans. You both must flee to find safety with Venutius. He will make a plan for your future."

She paused once again, lifting a piece of cheese from the nearby pouch. "You are princesses of a great Celtic tribe," she continued. "If you are taken captive, Rome will make an example of you, the symbol of subjugation upon our island."

She lifted her cheese, adding to it the roasted meat of a salted game bird, and a slab of wheat bread freshly baked in the early hours of the morn. As she ate, she urged her daughters to share the hearty bounty, finishing it off under the orange and magenta of the setting sun. Then, she drank from the flask, the waters still cool under the darkening sky. She passed the flask to Alaina and Valeda.

Mother and daughters sat in silence, watching the soft light of the new moon replace the brilliance of the sun as the stars began to fill the sky. Then, Boudicca spoke. "We must bed down for the night. Indomarius will send someone to rouse us before the dawn."

They gathered the remains of the food into the traveling pack, returning it to the chariot and unlashing the heavy woolen blankets meant for slumber. As they went, Boudicca looked long at Alaina and Valeda, the bloom of their youth swiftly cut off by the assault of an advancing Roman army. Valeda still slender and pale, the slight reddish hue of Alaina's cheeks barely a hint of her formerly ruddy countenance.

They rolled out the blankets upon the grasses, Boudicca covering them against the autumn chill. As they lay beneath the beech trees, listening to the rush of waters against the stony shore alongside them, they fell swiftly asleep.

Boudicca awoke with a start, her shoulders shaken gently by an urgent young warrior, kneeling at her side. "You must wake quickly, my queen," he said, as he stood, stepping aside to give her room to rise. "The Romans rumble within the walls of the temple, and Indomarius gathers both tribes to again encircle them." He turned, heading toward the mass of gathering warriors. Boudicca rose, waking Alaina and Valeda, quickly rolling the blankets to lash them once again inside the wicker wood chariot. Alaina let loose the ponies, holding them gently, stroking their nuzzles, leading them toward the chariot to harness.

Then, they drove toward the temple, the grasses still wet with dew, the first light of dawn breaking through the mist of the early morn. Indomarius had already led both tribes to circle the structure, tightly flanking it, and motioned her to bring the chariot alongside him, a symbol of tribal strength.

"The Romans stir inside the temple walls," he said. "But, they show no sign of coming forth to face the swords of our warriors."

"We shall wait," said Boudicca. "Our saddlebags hold the game of Iceni lands, and the waters of the river will quench our thirst." The sun rose in the sky, a bright, red ball, warming the backs of the warriors, and the long, shaggy manes of their mounts.

For two days, the Romans stood firm inside the walls, the Celts tightly about the temple. On the third day, with a downpour darkening the skies, and thunder drowning out the sounds of battle, the Romans poured forth, their swords raised, their helmets and breastplates intact.

But, with their training far behind them, and weak with hunger, the Celts cut them swiftly down, a waiting warrior attacking almost as instantly as they emerged. Those who refused to fight fled on foot to the nearby woods.

Slain Romans lay everywhere about the grassy plain, once the site of Claudian worship, the heavy rains of the downpour washing them clean. Cries of victory arose from the clusters of exhausted warriors. Boudicca rode about in her wicker wood chariot, praising their valor as she went.

"We have silenced the Roman enemy in Camulodunum," she shouted. "We shall take back our freedom to till our lands, reaping the bounty only for our own tables. To ride the plains and lift our swords only in our own defense."

"Now, we must get some rest," she added. "We leave for Londinium by sunrise."

As Boudicca bedded down for the night with Alaina and Valeda, the heavy downpour making the river rise, she thought of Venutius, safely harbored among the Cautevelanni, Caractacus, an exile in Rome, and Diviticus, so far away on the Isle of Mona. As her eyes closed in slumber, she prayed to Sequanna, and to Dagda and Morrigan, the Celtic gods of war, to protect the Iceni and Trinobantes warriors, and to bring them the victory they sought.

Chapter Twenty-One

Boudicca stood at the top of a hill, her hand above her brow, shading her eyes to view the valley below. Her warriors had sacked and plundered a number of smaller tribes with allegiance to the Romans, and had gathered a larger number who were bent on fighting for their freedom, swelling the numbers of Celtic warriors which now numbered in the thousands.

With victory behind them, and Seutonius and the Roman army headed for Mona to rid the island of the Druids, they had decided to attack Londinium, the largest city of the province, and a stronghold for Roman trade. Though densely populated, its occupants were unarmed, the hub of their activity centered on trade ships and merchants.

As Boudicca stood, she knew the valley below lay very near the thriving city built along the sea. A port to carry Celtic goods to Rome, crafted at the expense of the needs upon the island. Beautifully woven fabrics, jewelry made from the coral beneath the sea, urns of molded clay, goblets of gold and silver, tables and chairs chiseled from the oaks and maples of the Britons' woodlands. And, the swords and breastplates to protect an army of their oppressors.

She must meet with the chieftains of every tribe that joined them, and with her own council of Indomarius and her seasoned warriors. She must bring unity to tribes who once knew only independence, and with them lay out a plan of attack that would level Londinium and render it useless as a port along the Roman trade route.

As she walked the grasses of the hillside, lush with the brilliant gold of the autumn gorse and the pale lavender of the heather, she thought of Alaina and Valeda. She prayed to Sequanna to return to them the peace and the freedom of their childhood.

Then, she headed for the valley below, where the Celts had camped for three days to recover their strength and check their stores of food, flush with victory and anxious to push on to reclaim what was once a thriving Celtic stronghold. She found Indomarius monitoring the games of the young warriors who, with flagons of ale washing down the dried game and cheese, might easily have taken their valor to the death.

"We must call a meeting of council," she said. "We must take advantage of the distance of the Roman army and the distractions of the gladiator games and laden tables of Rome for Claudius and the Roman senate."

"I will round up our warriors and send our young Marinius here who tires of these games to call the chieftains to council," he answered, rising from the squatting position he had taken to better oversee the actions of the youths.

As Marinius left with instructions and a designated meeting place in a glade at the edge of a nearby forest, Indomarius and Boudicca strolled the plain, the scent of the newly budding primroses and violets filling the air as they walked.

Indomarius talked of his wife Delphia and his two daughters left behind. His two sons, both warriors, fighting by his side on a field of battle new to them, brought pride to his voice as he spoke.

As they reached the glade, they chose a fallen log to seat themselves upon, Boudicca arranging her simple earth tone course linen tunic, held by a wide circle of gold embossed with the Iceni crest, about her, waiting for the chiefs and her Iceni council to join them. She threw over it a crimson mantle, warding off the chill of the late autumn afternoon. As they sat, squirrels scurried beneath the trees, a red fox ran for cover, and an acorn, dropped from the mouth of a startled squirrel on a branch above them, fell nearly at their feet.

As the chiefs assembled, Boudicca fell silent, waiting for them to settle. They chose the soft, mossy ground, covered with pine needles, sitting cross-legged upon it.

When they were silent, Boudicca spoke. "I know you have never seen a woman upon the field of battle," she said, "But, the minstrels sing of two great queens who led their tribes to victory in battle."

She paused, looking at each chief as she stopped. Then, she continued. "But, I fight not as Iceni queen, but as an Iceni woman and daughter of the ancients. To avenge the wrongs of the Romans upon me and upon my daughters."

She paused once again, raising her voice over the clatter of the birds as she continued. "I will lead you to freedom," she said. "I will fight to the death as our ancestors fought before us."

"Now," she said, leaning forward to emphasize her words, "we must make a plan to sack Londinium. It is a large city, but we number now in the thousands. We must ride in, all of our tribes together, plundering what we see before us.

"But, we must also make a plan for a special group of warriors to ride at the same time toward the Roman governor's villa, destroying its stone walls and leveling all that's in it.

"Then, as we lay waste to Londinium, we must remove all food stores. Our warriors must stave their hunger, to keep their energy behind their desire to drive the Romans into the sea."

When she finished, Varix, chief of the Osismi, a small inland tribe, spoke. "Our warriors could lay waste to the governor's villa," he said, shifting his weight to a squatting position to be better heard by the others. "Before the Romans," he continued, "we sacked many a tribe who took by night our grain and our goats. Our warriors are fierce, and it took but one raid to destroy a thief."

The other chiefs, along with her Iceni warriors, nodded in assent, the reputation of Osismi raids legend upon the island.

Indomarius spoke next. "It is agreed," he said. "Varix will lead the Osismi to attack, laying waste the governor's villa, looting the great stores of grain taken in taxes from farmers who toil from the first rays of the sun to put bread on Roman tables, and routing the governor and his servants to face our sabers and our swords."

Then, Carvilius, chief of the Cenimagni, spoke. "Our warriors must attack riding only upon their mounts. We must leave our chariots, for the streets of Londinium are winding and narrow."

Murmurs of agreement followed. Boudicca answered. "I alone will remain upon my chariot, a symbol of Celtic victory."

Next, Taximagulus, chief of the Segontiaci, a tribe settled north along the sea, spoke. "We must ride in from all sides at once, to drive the enemy into the sea. We must attack the day of a full moon, for then the tide will be highest, the harbor vessels far from their reach. The enemy will be forced to face our swords and our javelins."

Carvilius, who had studied with the Druids of his tribe as a youth, then spoke. "Three days will bring a full moon into the evening sky," he said.

Boudicca, still seated upon the log, answered. "Three days will give our warriors rest and a chance to keep in practice their skills. Also, it will give us enough time to strike ahead of Claudius' notice, for he has shown us that our island is not now his first political concern. He sent merely two hundred soldiers in answer to the plea for reinforcements from the fleeing veterans of Camulodunum."

Indomarius, listening intently until now, spoke. "It is agreed we attack Londinium three days hence," he said. "We will lay a plan of attack that will allow the Osismi open passage to the Roman governor's villa while we ride the streets of the city to drive them toward the sea."

"Now," he continued, "go back to your tribes and share our plan of attack with your warriors. Tonight, we celebrate our victory at Camulodunum and along the east with a feast and games."

The chiefs rose to return to their tribal encampments, Indomarius and his council to return to the Iceni. As Boudicca and Indomarius walked the plain, Boudicca praised him for his skills in keeping the chiefs, the fierce, the independent, the mild, together to fight for the freedom of all Celts of the island. Then, she left, walking the fields to search for Alaina and Valeda.

The days before the planned attack of the city of Londinium gave Boudicca a chance to spend time with Alaina and Valeda. To roam the fields, walk the plains, and ride the surrounding forests on borrowed mounts. As they walked, the blooms of the knapweed, the campion and the honeysuckle, brought daily new scents wafting into the air around them. The sisters chased each other, engaging occasionally in a game of tag, chasing the butterflies flitting from bloom to bloom and the starlings and robins above them, their laughter filling the air about them. Alaina wove garlands of wildflowers, winding them through her sister's tresses, bringing a ruddy glow to Valeda's otherwise pale countenance.

They took their meals beside a stream in the woodland, catching a speckled trout or two to cook for their evening meal. Boudicca prayed with her daughters to Sequanna, asking for blessings for their future joinings, using the rites she learned as a youth from Diviticus, and a rough-hewn idol she carved from a sturdy branch of a nearby oak.

On the last night, they sat around their campfire, the stars shining bright in a clear, dark sky, their features lit by a nearly full moon. Alaina spoke. "Mama," she asked, "how shall we ride tomorrow?"

Boudicca answered, looking at her daughter's sinewy frame, toughened from seasons of riding the plains and the woodlands with Nerthus. "Alaina, you will drive the ponies," she said, "keeping them running as fast as you can after we charge the city."

Then, she looked at Valeda, slender and wan, pale since the attack on the palace, losing her morning meal almost faster than she could eat it. "Valeda," she said, more softly, "you will raise the Iceni crest, keeping it high so our warriors might look upon it as they crush the Romans and drive them into the sea."

As Boudicca finished, Alaina rose, pulling blankets from the saddlebags of their tethered mounts. They lay upon them in silence, pondering the brilliance of the more prominent stars, the still of the night broken only by the chirping of a cricket or two. Then, mother and daughters fell into slumber beneath the newly leafed branches of the moonlit trees.

The day of the attack on Londinium brought torrents of spring rains pouring from the skies. The tribes were assembled, breaking camp and gathering as one, each tribe led by their chief, the Iceni brought together by Indomarius. Boudicca stood before them, tall in her wicker wood chariot, her many-hued mantle bright despite the grey of the day, her large, golden torque, emblazoned with the Iceni crest, glistening through the mist.

As she stood, she motioned for the minstrels to sound the horns of battle, giving the signal to begin. As they rode, she paced them, saving the energy of the warriors for the battle ahead. As the stone of the shops and homes of Londinium rose before them, she raised her arm in signal to attack.

Hordes of Celts, flush with the victory of the eastern seaboard, and bent with the urge to regain the freedom they once knew, some clad in tunics girded with gold and silver, large torques above them, others naked with the dye of the woad plant upon them, all with the iron helmets of battle topped with the horns of the stag and the boar, or the fierce birds of the woodlands, charged the unwalled city. Inhabitants, unarmed for the last many years, scurried for cover. The Romans searched for their weapons, laid carelessly about since Roman rule had been imposed upon the city.

Panic arose on both sides. The mud of the narrow, dirt streets captured the hooves of the Celtic mounts, forcing a number of warriors to dismount and fight on foot. The torrents of waters racing down the cobblestone streets caused their mounts to slide.

"Alaina, stay to the cobblestone roads," shouted Boudicca, as Alaina urged the ponies forward, pulling a chariot meant to travel the grassy plains. "We will be done if the mud puts a stop to the wheels of our chariot."

"Stay as far ahead of our warriors as you can," she continued, shouting above the noise of battle. "If anyone attacks us, our warriors are sworn to protect us before they turn to slaying the enemy or defending themselves."

"Valeda," she called, shouting as well, "hold high our Iceni crest. We fight for the cause of Celtic freedom."

As she spoke, the noise of battle grew louder, the minstrels having exchanged their horns for swords, the warriors on foot in hand to hand combat with Romans who had no time to form a protective phalanx, some who had lost their swords to a well-trained Roman swordsman, using their fierceness to escape the sword of an opponent and sink the dagger they pulled from its scabbard behind a protective Roman breastplate.

The warriors still on their mounts had the advantage, and used it well. They rode protection for the warriors on foot, leaning to knock the sword out of the hand of a menacing Roman swordsman.

Despite the chaos of the battle, the Romans were clearly outnumbered. The ferocity of the Celts and the surprise attack which had forced the Romans to abandon their well-trained discipline of defense, took its toll upon them. Those who were not slain were easily forced by the mounted Celts in the direction of the sea.

As they fought, the Osismi charged quickly the Roman governor's villa, the stone of its indoor and outdoor baths surrounded by steam from the vessels of heated waters, its courtyards lush with the greenery and multi-colored blooms of well-tended gardens.

The governor and his family, clad in the togas of his political office, sat at table, dining on the fruit, the grains, the cheeses, the game, and ales of the surrounding countryside and the choicest figs and olives and wines shipped daily from the nearby continent. A bevy of slaves, taken during the fall of Londinium, hovered nearby, sensitive to the family's slightest whim, shown by the frequent snap of a pair of fingers.

As they sat, the Osismi surrounded the villa, tightly encircling it with the depth of several warriors. No gates blocked their entrance, so certain were the Romans of their absolute rule.

Varix called out, but his shouts were met only with chaos from within. Then, he gave the signal to storm the doors, now bolted from the inside by a cadre of Roman soldiers housed at the rear of the villa to keep order within the city and to urge the farmers in the surrounding countryside should they offer resistance to part with their increasingly rising taxes.

The heavy, wooden doors gave way to Osismi axes, the shuttered windows to the blows of well-placed clubs. As they stormed the villa, they overpowered the soldiers, barred from escape at every exit, and, over the frenzied shouts of protest from the governor as he rose from table with threats of retaliation from

Rome, put into shackles the governor and his family, driving them into the streets and toward the sea.

"You will not get away this," he shouted, his pudgy countenance bristling with a mixture of terror and aggravation. "Claudius will crush you, Rome will retaliate, and Rome will be victorious forever."

Varix, tall on his mount, shouted back. "We Celts are free people. We have done nothing to you Romans. You take our lands. You take our crops. You take our women. We shall fight to the death to ride the plains of our lands again in freedom and to defend the honor of our ancestors."

As they went, Roman soldiers fled before them, hoping for a chance of escape in the vessels that were anchored along the sea, passing the shackled family. As they reached the shore, Boudicca's chariot stood before them, her presence imposing as she stood before her warriors, ordering them to slay every Roman or drive them into the sea. Many of the Romans, some with hastily clad breastplates or leather armlets, most by now without weapons, ran toward the sea, only to be driven back by the force of the evening tide, to be cut down by a Celtic sword. Others pulled under by the strength of the waters and the great waves rushing toward the shore.

As Varix reached the rocks of the shore, he gave the governor a choice of the sea or an Osismi sword. The governor, choosing the sea and dragging his family after him toward the ships, now rocking ever more violently in the harbor, sank with the rising tide and the iron of their shackles, allowing the sea to claim them.

As the battle came to an end, Boudicca spoke to the warriors gathered about her. "We must loot every dwelling, for we will be unable to sow the crops of spring. We must store the grain to bake bread to give us sustenance to meet our foe."

"Each tribe will take a turn to keep watch and bring order to the city," she continued. "The rest will camp just beyond the city streets."

The celebration of victory lasted two days and two nights, with plenty of ale and games and wild boar on roasted spits. But, many of the warriors, both young and old, far from their women and their fields, now left untended, began to give way to flagging spirits. Boudicca sighed as she thought of how to bring back the fight that brought them from their homes to Camulodunum.

As she pondered the question, the second night of revelry just getting underway with the rise of a sliver of a moon, Valeda came upon her. Her long, blond tresses glimmering in the soft moonlight, the flush of her cheeks made vibrant by the blaze of a nearby torch.

"Mama", she said, "why is my middle so big when I lose nearly all of my morning meal?"

Boudicca looked at her daughter, her tunic draped loosely about her, her face as pale as the snow upon the winter's hillsides. She had been too preoccupied to notice Valeda's changing shape.

She pulled Valeda to her, holding her about the shoulders as she brought her to walk beside her toward the nearby hillside. Then, she sat upon it, pulling her daughter down beside her on the slightly damp grasses of evening. "You must rest," she said. "I will comb the woodlands on the morrow for a plant that will help you ward off your morning sickness."

"Now," she continued, "we will find a spot away from the revelers full of ale, and lay our blankets beneath the branches of a tree. We will sing the songs of your childhood, and we will count the stars until we fall into slumber beneath the sky. And, tomorrow, as the sun's rays wake us, we shall talk."

She rose, taking Valeda by the hand as she spoke, heading for a stand of trees not far from a nearby lake. As they went, Boudicca shuddered as she thought of how she would tell her daughter she was with child.

Chapter Twenty-Two

Seutonius Paulinus surveyed the waters that stood between his army on Briton's mainland and the isle of Mona. A host of barbarians awaited him on the other side, fierce warriors protective of the Druids who had fled there. Long a refuge for fugitives from everywhere, the group included some of the fiercest warriors of the island and the Continent, many of them independent warriors for hire.

Seutonius, famed for his knowledge of military strategy and skills, knew he must conquer them and rid the island of the holy men who had brought belief in a higher order and a desire to do battle in honor of their ancestors to the barbarians of the island. He knew, also, that to beat his biggest rival, the great general Corbulo, who had subdued Armenia for Rome, or to best his predecessors, Aulius Didius, who had kept the already subjugated tribes at bay, but never conquered new ones, or Veranius, who died before he ravaged any further than a few raids upon the Silures, he would have to subjugate the entire island of Briton, turning it into a province of Rome.

The waters that stood between the barbarians and his army were uncertain, shallow at one point, the floor of the ocean rising and falling with no apparent pattern, deep at another. The vessels they had brought would never carry them to the other side, grounding his soldiers and their mounts, creating chaos and keeping them from the rush of meeting their foe.

Seutonius called for an aide, the leader of the Praetorian Guard, Marcus Aurelius. When he arrived, Seutonius dismounted, handing the reins of his black stallion to a waiting slave. "We must talk," he said, as Aurelius dismounted as well. "We must make a plan to cross the water, lest our army get caught in the shallows, trapping our mounts as well."

Aurelius silently surveyed the water, the glint of the noonday sun upon it, the schools of fish and the sea urchins visible beneath the brilliant hues of blues and greens. He waited, knowing Seutonius would soon lay out a plan, for not only did the general's military skills surpass all others, he rarely listened to the council of a subordinate.

After a lengthy pause, Seutonius continued. "We will build flat-bottomed boats to carry our infantry across the water to the other shore," he said. "Our cavalry will ford the shallows on the backs of their horses, and swim the depths alongside their mounts."

Aurelius turned toward Seutonius, gazing for a moment at the tall, lean sinewy frame, impeccably clad in formal military garb, a small mustache grazing his upper lip, his locks graying slightly at the temples cropped short. "We will begin immediately to forage for the wood to build our boats," he said. "We have just ridden past woodlands that stretch far inland. I will send our best boat builders out to the forest to find the wood that will give our vessels strength, accompanied by men handiest with the axe."

"But, now we must rest," he said. "We have ridden long and hard this day. We will begin at sunrise to cut and measure our planks."

"Now, I must get back to my men," he continued. "Despite the crudeness of camp, far from the streets of Rome, the Guard expects its privileges. I must arrange for field games and prizes, a banquet of the best fish and game our slaves can manage to prepare, and a lavish flow of ale."

As he finished speaking, he climbed his mount, leaving Seutonius to contemplate a strategy that would get his army to the shore of Mona, and win a battle against a very large band of fugitives and warriors for hire.

The games of the Praetorian Guard lasted into the night, torches lighting the revelry, the midnight air carrying the sounds of cheers for Roman victories, both winners and losers passing out onto the bedrolls of tents set up by slaves, to sober up by morning. The men of the regular army were doled as much as could be expended of the dwindling rations, collapsing onto blankets set out under the open sky in the chilly night air of late autumn.

The boat building began the next morning, slaves laying planks of oak and maple and ash end to end to form the flat bottom of a boat. The rounded sides were made as usual, the inside filled with seats for the slaves who oared the boat and seats alongside for the foot soldiers.

The cavalry groomed their horses and the foot soldiers practiced their swordplay. The Praetorian Guard ironed out the drunken fights from the night before, and did exercises to maintain their riding and swordsmanship skills.

Seutonius sat alone in his tent, thinking of the military genius of Caesar and the generals who had gone before him, plotting outside in the dirt a proper military landing, slaves bringing in his food and water. Every now and then he called in an aide to bounce his ideas off of.

"We must get the infantry across all at once," he said to Lucius Pompeius who, beckoned, sat nearby on a stool at the edge of the tent. "The barbarians will be waiting in all their strength, throwing javelins to keep us from the shore. The infantry is better prepared to resist them. The cavalry must concern themselves with the welfare of their mounts. The infantry must engage the barbarians with swords while the cavalry swims ashore."

Lucius Pompeius said nothing, nodding as Seutonius spoke. When he finished, Pompeius answered. "I will give the command to Gaius Decianus. He will prepare the infantry to dodge the javelins and prepare for a quick attack once they reach shore."

Seutonius continued. "The infantry must divert the attention of the barbarians, to allow the cavalry to land. But, once ashore, the cavalry must take quick action, for the cavalry of the barbarians will first have the advantage, and they are trained by nature, for their horses are not bound by the limits of a city, and they ride hills and woodlands year round."

As Seutonius finished, Pompeius stood. "I will call a meeting with Decianus and Cassius Octavianus of the cavalry. They will coordinate a plan that will get the infantry across and the cavalry just behind them."

As Pompeius left, Seutonius walked out of the tent and toward the large area set aside to split the wood felled by the expert axmen. The sounds of boat building filled the air, slaves with mallets striking the wood, others fashioning the planks, some off to the side carving the pegs, many former boat builders themselves.

In the tents of the Praetorian Guard, Marcus Quintillius Calenus sat on the edge of his bedroll, his few possessions still in a small pack he had carried from Rome. The assurances of his centurion Fabius Antonius, that the Guard would be back in Rome shortly after an attack on Londinium and a short stint on the Britons' isle, had faded into the distance. His nights of gaming and chasing women, trading tales of military glory, seemed farther away after seasons of battle with tribes who refused to submit.

He reread the worn letters of his father, his only tie to home. As he sat, Lucius Varinius, a tent mate, came in, putting his hand on Marcus' shoulder, then beckoning him to join him for a stroll along the rocky banks of the ocean. As they walked, the scent of salt water filled the air, the sound of the waves lent a power to the still of the early spring afternoon, hung heavy with fog.

As they walked, Varinius, a career soldier, spoke. "We have been long gone from Rome," he said, "and I miss my family and the villas of my family and friends. The banquets far into the night, the taverns, the feasts of the finest meats and fruits and wines. But, we will add to the glory of the empire when we conquer this island, and riches will flow into Rome."

"I think the sooner we conquer, the sooner we will back on the streets of Rome," returned Marcus, "with the flow of wine and ale, and slave girls to fill your goblets. This island is hostile, rocky, thick with rain and fog." He paused. "Do you have a wife, Lucius?" he asked.

Varinius walked a distance, then answered. "I am engaged to a woman of a well-born family, Varinnia Lapidus. She is beautiful.

Her long, dark hair falls almost to her waist, and when she is gay, the room lights up with her laughter. She will wait for me. And, when we finish this campaign, the sounds of merrymaking and the toasts of our wedding will fill the streets of Rome."

"My sister is now of age for marriage," said Marcus. "I wonder who she will marry."

"Perhaps it will not be long before you find the answer," said Lucius. "Seutonius is a good general. Harsh, but bent on finally subduing this island for the empire. He will achieve his goal."

As the two walked along the rocky edge of the ocean, musing upon their own thoughts, the sun sank slowly into the horizon of the sea.

As Seutonius satisfied himself that the vessels, enough to hold the entire infantry, would soon be done, he returned to his tent. Every victory brought him closer to the recognition he should have had long ago, he mused, if only Corbulo had not been so successful in subduing Armenia. He sat down to refine the plan of attack on Mona.

On a late autumn morning, sixty flat-bottom boats bearing the infantrymen of the legion under Seutonius set out for the shores of Mona. Slaves oared the boats, trying to stay free of the shallows that slowed their speed.

Seutonius led the fleet, sitting at the helm surrounded by standard bearers and the most expert javelin throwers and swordsmen of the legion. The infantry, dressed in full battle regalia, sat erect, iron helmets with red feather crests upon them, leather breastplates covering their identical white tunics, leather leg protectors, wood and leather shields with golden Roman insignia by their sides.

The cavalry followed, their battle gear stowed in a pack upon their mounts, close at hand to don as they neared the shores of Mona. The relative calm of the sea provided an ease for the oarsmen, their synchronized strokes propelling them forward with the greatest of speed. The grey of the day, thick with fog, provided cover.

As they rowed, bands of warriors lined the shores of Mona, standing several rows deep. Some with their naked bodies covered by the dye of the woad plant, depicting the gods of their tribes or the frightful images of their imagination. Others, covered by simple tunics, their iron helmets sporting bronze and golden birds and horns, their shields the length of their bodies, studded with coral and etched with the birds and the stags of the woodlands.

Druids stood nearby, waving their arms toward the sky, shouting powerful incantations. Women with disheveled tresses and long, black tunics, ran screaming amongst the warriors.

The sight, unfamiliar to the eye of a Roman, brought panic to the boats as they moved forward, rendering many of the well-trained infantrymen limp with fright. Seutonius stood, keeping his balance over the swell of the waves. "You men quail before a group of frenzied women," he shouted. "Return to your senses and remember your army training. Keep your ranks close for the barbarians fight with a passion but without a well-trained order. Alight, and bring glory to the Roman empire." At that, he sat, pushing his standard bearers, still mute with fright, to wade ashore, giving the order to the infantry to follow.

Once ashore, the massacre was complete. Outnumbered, and unused to organized battle, the Celts, though strong with fury, fell to the superior military strength of the Roman army. The Druids, untrained in swordsmanship, were cut down quickly as well. "Now," shouted Seutonius, "run through with a sword every woman who has aided the battle, or who runs or flees."

As the bodies lay upon the field of battle, Seutonius set up a command to destroy the sacred groves of the Druids. The stone temples were smashed to rubble, the wooden altars, set among the hawthorns and the ash trees, and the wooden cages where the sacred hares and nightingales were kept, were set ablaze with the very torches the Celts had used to keep the Romans from their shores.

The annihilation complete, Seutonius prepared the return trip to the mainland. Boats were salvaged, slaves were set to clean the silt and the mud, and the wounded were laid on the floors of the largest vessels.

As the boats were oared back to camp, over the now rougher waters of evening, Seutonius asked Decianus to prepare a victory celebration for the legion, one that would last several days. "The legion deserves it," he said, as he turned to the career soldier who was one of his top aides. "They have fought hard and well. We must give them rest, and a boost to their morale. We have destroyed the last of the barbarians' priests. Their only link to the law and order of their tribes, and to what they believe are their ancestors' spirits who give them courage in battle."

As Seutonius' vessel neared shore, he climbed over the sides of his boat to wade ashore, giving the infantrymen amusement and a signal to do the same. As he stood ashore, his sandals wet with salt water, the waves of the evening tide behind him growing louder with every rush, a messenger ran out from a nearby tent. "General Seutonius," he said, "I bear a message from the emperor."

"The emperor will be pleased with our victory," returned Seutonius. "I will give you the news for your return journey."

As he spoke, the infantrymen walked around him, anxious to return to their stores of ale and a bed. "I'm afraid the news is bad," answered the messenger. "The emperor has asked I give it as soon as I come upon you. He asks as well you act upon it immediately."

Seutonius' body stiffened, his eyes turning intently upon the messenger. "What is the news," he asked.

"There has been an insurrection to the south," continued the messenger. "A woman, Boudicca, queen of the Iceni tribe, leads the barbarians. She seeks revenge for an attack upon her and her daughters by our veterans after the death of her husband, Prasutagus. They have sacked Londinium and Verulamium. They take no prisoners as slaves, but destroy all in their path."

"You have delivered your message," answered Seutonius. "Now, go to the tent of Octavianus. He will see that you are fed and given rest."

Then, he walked directly toward his tent. As he entered it, he removed his sandals and his tunic, exchanging them for dry ones, declining an invitation to join the festivities being set up all around him. As he dressed, he thought how Prasutagus had been given everything by Rome. And, how could the barbarians follow a woman? He sat down promptly upon a small wooden stool set before a table with a stylus and began to devise a plan to crush the insubordinate rebels.

Chapter Twenty-Three

Boudicca stood at the edge of a field filled with the poppies, the hawk weed, the corn daisies, and the newly bleached grasses of autumn. Black, green and gold-plumed pheasants and coveys of partridges moved among them. Small hills rose behind her, a valley stretched below, a river flowed beside it. The songs of the thrush, the skylarks and the wren, nested in the red and golden-leafed branches of the elm, the birch and the maple, their nests now empty of fledglings, wafted up through the breeze from the valley below.

It had been long since she had ridden the plains and woodlands for pleasure with Alaina and Valeda. Long since they had tethered their mounts to share their childhood tales over an evening meal beneath the leaves of an oak tree.

The ranks of the Celtic warriors who had chosen to follow Boudicca had swelled to over 40,000. With three major victories behind them, and unused to long absences from home, the warriors of most of the tribes that had joined them had sent for their women. Wagonsful had arrived in the last several weeks, putting the encampment into a perpetual state of reunions, laundry and occasional general merriment.

Valeda grew larger every day, the pallor of her countenance growing ruddier as she walked in the noonday sun or sat upon a rock in the rays of the morning sun to dress her tresses. Both Boudicca and Alaina encouraged her to eat, roasting special tidbits of freshly caught fish over an open fire during their evening meal, saving for her the freshest chunks of oaten or wheat bread baked from the ransacked spoils of battle. And, throwing a woolen mantle about her to keep her from the chill of the rain and the fog.

Boudicca had news that Seutonius was traveling south to meet them, livid at the destruction of Londinium, Rome's largest island port. Her scouts kept watch on his progress, reporting to her every day. She must meet with Indomarius and her council. A victory would change the minds of the Trinobantes, the largest Roman-held tribe on the island's eastern coast, to join them.

As she mused on the politics of battle, she thought of Diviticus. Diviticus who only asked to bring the wisdom of the gods and the skies to the people of the Coritani tribe, to intervene on behalf of peace, to take a maiden to his knee to fill her young head with the hopes and the dreams of the ancients.

She thought of Diviticus lying slain on the beaches of Mona. She hoped that his journey to the Other World would be one of peace, and when he reached his destination, he would impart his wisdom forever.

As Boudicca passed through her thoughts, she heard behind her a rustling in the tall, brown grasses, giving way to a familiar hearty laughter. She turned to see Linnea running toward her, barefoot across the meadow, arms outstretched, her simple, pale green linen tunic flowing in the midday breeze.

As Linnea reached her, they threw their arms about each other, holding a long embrace, the memories of their long friendship crossing their thoughts at once. "Oh, Linnea," said Boudicca, as they parted their embrace, "how did you get here?"

"It was a long journey," answered Linnea, "but I knew I must join Anthropus. I have left the fields in the hands of Anthropus' father, and the care of the children to his mother and to mine."

"Yes," Boudicca said, "Anthropus has been gone long. Mandorix sent the Coritani to us soon after the victory at Camulodunum."

"Our fields do not give what they gave when Anthropus was there to till them," said Linnea. "Though we work from when the sun's rays begin to fall upon our shutters, and finish when the moon begins to rise, neither I nor the children can pull from the earth what he can."

"And, how do the children now number?" asked Boudicca.

"Five hungry mouths now fill our dwelling," said Linnea, a broad smile, much like the one that crossed her features in childhood as they sat cross-legged upon the gorse along the Coritani river banks watching the frogs jump for insects and the squirrels at play, broke out about the creases of her now worn countenance.

"I must get back to Anthropus," she continued, "for his garments are in sore need of cleaning."

"You would be very proud of Anthropus, Linnea," said Boudicca. "He has used his courage well. He has held the faith of our ancestors in battle and polished his skills with our ancient warriors as we camp."

"May the gods be with you, Boudicca," said Linnea. "I shall pray to Sequanna to give to our children the peace we knew as maidens along the fields and woodlands of the Coritani."

"I must also embrace Alaina and Valeda," she added, "for I have not gazed upon them since they newly learned to walk across the Iceni fields and chase the balls we threw them."

She then embraced Boudicca once again, turning at parting toward the Celts' encampment, her steps a little less lively than those of her youth, her shoulders bent forward slightly with the mantle of worry.

As she left, Boudicca headed toward camp to search for Indomarius. They must set a plan to meet Seutonius and his army.

Indomarius sat in a glade not far from the edge of camp, a stool set out for him to support his weary frame. Boudicca sat nearby on a bench, her long, red tresses held back by a single, linen strand, her simple, green linen tunic edged with golden Iceni crests gathered neatly about her, her worn feet covered by sandals of doe-skin, her attention on the chiefs and the ancient warriors of her council sitting cross-legged about her on the tufts of grass competing for the rays of the sun in the only clearing of the dense woodland.

Boudicca spoke. "Seutonius rides to meet us in battle as the crow flies, stopping only at Londinium to survey the damage. Our scouts report he has refused to spare his army to give aid to the city, so anxious is he to meet us."

"We must not attack another city or outpost," she continued, as she leaned forward to be better heard above the chirping of the birds flitting about among the trees at the edge of the glade. "We must save our strength to defeat Seutonius. A victory will convince the Trinobantes, who have not been hasty to break their Roman oppression, to join us."

"We are camped now in the open, far from the gates of a city," she added. "But, if we hold ourselves within a city's gates, or a woodland, or our backs to a river or a set of hills, we make ourselves vulnerable to Seutonius and his army.

"We now outnumber the Romans. Claudius sends them no replacements, thinking our efforts of little value."

Varix, still triumphant with the flush of victory at Londinium, spoke next. "Our tribes are ready to face the Romans," he said, as he changed to a squatting position to be better heard. "We polish our skills in practice each morn as the sun comes up and in games at evening by the light of the torch. Our young warriors learn well from the ancients covered with the scars of battle who teach them."

Carvilius spoke next. "Our Cenimagni warriors are ready as well, anxious to cut down the Roman army. They fight for the women who have joined them, and for the freedom and honor of their homes and their tribal lands."

"Seutonius has the advantage in choice of battle field," said Boudicca, addressing all the chiefs at once. "He will not attack us here in the open, because he knows he is outnumbered. He knows, also, that we must destroy him in order to gain the freedom of our island. He counts on the destruction of the Druids to throw us into panic, making us easy prey to a final Roman submission. We must avenge the deaths of our Druids, and take back the freedom which is ours." She paused, leaning back upon her bench. She continued. "We must wait for Seutonius to choose a site, and then devise a plan to overrun his army."

The chiefs agreed, nodding and murmuring their assent. As they finished, they rose to return to their women and their sword and javelin bouts, Boudicca calling for a large celebration and as much feasting as they could spare, to raise the spirits of their warriors so far from home. As they left, Boudicca headed back to camp to search for Alaina and Valeda.

She found them watering the ponies at a stream near to the oak trees they had chosen to slumber beneath, the sheltering branches reminding Boudicca of the seasons she had spent with Diviticus learning her duty and the lore he had time to teach her. As she came upon them, Alaina called out. "Mama, look yonder," she laughed, as she pointed to a bullfrog croaking loudly and hopping from stone to stone. "The ponies shy away, wondering what he is about," she said. "When Nerthus was a young mount, he played for hours with the bullfrogs in the stream beneath the meadows, the sun warming our backs as he went."

Boudicca laughed, following the antics of the bullfrog, as the ponies whinnied and tried to nudge him, and he quickly hopped out of the reach of their muzzles.

"We can take a stroll," she said, as she joined them at the river's edge, "perhaps along the water, where we can pluck the fruit of the elderberry and the crab-apple overhanging its banks, or through the woodlands, where we can catch a glimpse of the hares skittering about beneath the toadstools, or gather some mushrooms to liven the game of our evening meal."

They tethered the ponies, strolling slowly along the river's edge, its waters winding toward the middle of a woodland, the rays of the afternoon sun warming them as they went.

"Mama," asked Alaina, "when must we go to battle again?"

"We will wait until Seutonius rides to meet us," said Boudicca. "Then, we will face the Roman army. It may be a fortnight till they reach us."

"Until then," she continued, "we must rest, to conserve our strength and gather more. We must catch fish and hunt for game to add to our stores which rapidly grow less. We have had no time to reap our crops or to plow our fields to sow new ones."

"Mama, will there be games this evening by torchlight?" asked Valeda, her steps slowing as her breaths became more measured.

"Yes," said Boudicca, "our warriors must keep up their skills. And, we must be there to encourage them, and to applaud their valor with the javelin and the sword."

As they strolled, Alaina thought of Galorin, of the Osismi tribe. He had showed his courage at Londinium. He was strong, and his light brown locks reminded her of a wheat field on a sunny afternoon, the stalks and beards caught frantically in the gusts of an afternoon breeze. She must try and stand next to him at the jousts, for perhaps he would favor her with a glance, or even a word.

As they strolled, chatting as only a mother and daughters can chat, the image of Galorin slowly eclipsed all of Alaina's youthful thoughts.

Chapter Twenty-Four

As the first rays of the sun beat down upon the branches of the trees in the Mandeussedum forest, where most of the Iceni and their allies were camped, Boudicca and Indomarius gathered together all the tribal chiefs. Boudicca, clad in her helmet, a tunic of many hues gathered together with a belt of golden squares, each depicting an animal of the woodland, a wide golden torque with the Iceni crest about her neck which caught the rays of the sun, a long sword by her side, rode in the rear of her wicker wood chariot, Alaina and Valeda at the helm. Indomarius rode on the back of a freshly groomed roan, the chiefs on mounts of their choice, all watered and fed, rested and groomed the night before.

Seutonius had chosen a site for battle not far from where they were camped, a huge plain surrounded by hills and ravines and backed by a very thick forest, entered only by a narrow path between the hills and ravines. The Celts, with rapidly swelling forces, were now ready to attack. Their women would travel with them, set off to the side in wagons drawn by oxen, to watch the victory.

Boudicca went about from chief to chief, standing tall in the back of her chariot, drawn by the now refreshed ponies, shouting encouragement as she went. "Our tribes number four times Seutonius' army," she said. "Thus far, neither age nor virginity has been safe from the lust of Roman power."

"But, the gods are on the side of a righteous vengeance," she continued. "A Roman legion has perished at Camulodunum. The rest are in hiding or planning to flee. The Romans will fear the noise of our charge, and will never recover from the blows of our attack." She paused, then added, "If you live, you will be taken as slaves. You must conquer, or die."

Then, she rode to the front, the tribes assembling behind her, each led by their chief. She stood, facing the multitude. "Mounted warriors must stay to the side, to allow our warriors on foot to crush the Roman foot soldiers, who we outnumber three to one. Now, we must ride." She gave the signal.

As they rode through the meadows and plains of Mandeussedum, under a nearly cloudless sky, the clatter of horses' hooves echoed among the hillsides, the oak, the maple and the elm trees cleared of robins, the thrush and the sparrow, in flight from a noise that had sounded like strange thunder. The tiger lilies, the wild rose, the sunflowers crushed beneath them.

They rode as only the disenfranchised could ride, bent on recovering the freedom and lands that once were theirs. As they neared the battlefield, Boudicca signaled a halt, turning to face them as they pulled in their mounts to a stop.

"Seutonius has chosen an entry for us over a narrow path, below steep hills and above deep, rocky ravines," she shouted. "We must enter with no more than two or three at a time or we risk the loss of the footing of our mounts."

"Warriors on mounts go first, then warriors on foot, and last the women in our oxen-drawn wagons" she continued. "When we are assembled, facing Seutonius and his legions on the large plain of battle, the horn blowers will give the signal to charge."

At that, she signaled Alaina to begin entry onto the field of battle through the winding path. As they rode, stones and pebbles falling into the ravines below, she thought of how she must avenge the attack upon her daughters and herself, and how she must make it safe for Venutius to leave the harbor of the Catuvellauni.

As they entered the plain, they assembled to face a Roman army already in formation. Legions in a phalanx formation, arm to arm, more lightly armed and therefore more agile foot soldiers about them, and a densely arrayed cavalry on the sides. Seutonius rode up and down before them, confident in their military prowess, shouting encouragement as he went.

"The barbarians spew empty threats and bring their women with them," he said. "They are no match for a disciplined Roman army. It is a greater glory to be outnumbered and achieve a victory. Think only of destruction, not plunder, and victory, power and glory will be yours."

As he spoke, he rode in front of the foot soldiers. "Prepare to hurl the javelins," he said, "and finish the destruction with shield and with sword." Then, he gave the signal to begin.

At that, Boudicca signaled the horn blowers to sound the noise of battle, the din and the cacophony mixing with the shouts and the cries of attacking warriors. The Romans, mindful of their formation, closed ranks, the legion advancing as a wedge, throwing the hordes of Celts to the sides to be cut down by the more agile Roman swordsmen. The cavalry, evenly matched, traded blows sword to sword.

As they fought, muscles honed from seasons of riding the island's plains and tilling its fields nearly burst from the naked and nearly naked bodies of the Celtic warriors. But, panic ensued, the Romans held fast, and those who tried to flee to help their women were cut down or stopped by the wagons blocking the entry path.

Despite the panic, Linnea withdrew to the sidelines to keep her eye on Anthropus, his newly-learned skills put to the test with a number of agile Roman swordsmen. But, despite his courage, his throat was slit by a Roman on mount as he bent to help a warrior he had known since childhood.

Linnea flew to his side, but he had drawn his last gasp of air before she reached him. She rocked him as she held him, sobbing. As she knelt, the thrust of a Roman sword put an end to her own life as well. She fell, crushing the tall grasses beneath her, beside the Coritani farmer she had hoped she would be joined to since maidenhood.

Boudicca, drained by battle and the loss of thousands of warriors, retreated to the edge of the plain to survey the damage. As she fought off a number of approaching Roman soldiers, Alaina and Valeda guided the ponies to the rear of the battle field, the edge of a forest thickly treed with ancient oak and maples, elm and hawthorn.

She surveyed the plain, once filled with tall green grasses turned brown with the chill of autumn. Piles of bodies, warriors, women and oxen, lay intermingled, the scarlet of blood, much of it now dried and matted, some of it still gushing and oozing from lifeless bodies, now turning cold, had replaced the green of the plain.

Without her warriors, she would surely be taken captive. Paraded through the streets of Rome, a shackled trophy, a symbol of Roman valor and Celtic defeat. She shouted to Alaina and Valeda, "We must retreat to the woodland behind us. We must be quick, for we must use the cover of battle."

As she spoke, she jumped from the chariot, Alaina and Valeda behind her. As they made their way, the woods darkened, sunlight flickering through the heavily leafed branches, once the walkways of scampering squirrels and the perches of birds in flight. As they searched for a path, the patches of sky and sun grew fewer.

Boudicca woke to the shouting of her name, her unconsciousness broken only by a determined shaking. She lay beneath an oak tree, the stark, white berries of the mistletoe entwining it lay about her, some still clutched in the tight grip of her hand, the sap of those she ingested still clinging to her lips, now tightly pursed. Through the haze, she recognized a long familiar face, kept from her for many seasons past, the long, dark locks around it now turning slightly grey, the mustache above the strong, trim lips still a vibrant ebon.

"Venutius," she said, her voice sounding like an echo to her ears, "am I in the Other World?"

"No," the form, still blurred to her gaze, answered. "We are in the Mandeussedum forest, and you have just been in battle with the Romans."

"Venutius," she said, her voice weakening with each breath as she spoke, "how did you get here?"

"I could no longer desert you, Boudicca," he answered. "The Catuvellauni have been good to me. They gave me safe haven, when other tribes feared the power and the wrath of Cartimandua. I helped them govern, to stand as best we could against the encroaching power of the Romans."

He paused, shifting slightly to cradle her head in his arms. Then, he continued. "When I heard you were to meet Seutonius, I knew I must fight alongside you. But, I could not send you word. The Romans blocked all entry to your camp."

"I reached you by night," he added, "traveling by way of the stars as Diviticus taught. As I neared your camp, I met with the rear of your warriors as you rode to meet Seutonius."

"Venutius," she said, as she waited for him to finish his tale, "Alaina and Valeda are with me."

"I have found them," he answered. "I keep them hidden in safety."

She gasped, as the poison of the mistletoe began to erode her body. "I shall soon be journeying to the Other World," she said, her voice growing weaker, the glimmer of sunlight above them fading as she spoke. "Where crystal trees will sparkle before our gaze, the scent of blossoms will fill the air, and love will flourish forever."

"I shall meet you there," he answered, as he struggled to keep her head from the moss of the forest's floor, her long, red tresses entangled about the strength of his arms. As he spoke, the haze grew thicker to her sight, her eyelids closed over the blue of her once vibrant eyes.

Venutius, whose voice she could no longer hear, bent down, kissing her eyelids, then softly, her lips. Then, he laid her gently upon the mossy earth.

Chapter Twenty-Five

Venutius sat on a simple, wooden bench in the meadow behind a small dwelling fashioned from the stone of a nearby riverbed and erected with the wet, rich clay of the soil around it. His locks, now mostly grey, fell well below his shoulders. His simple linen tunic and trousers kept him from the slight chill of the gentle, spring winds. A single tree grew in the meadow beyond him. Hills, lush with greenery almost sparkling in the sun, rose nearby. As he sat, he chiseled, his newly sharpened carving knife fashioning a warrior from the block of maple he held upon his knees.

Nearby, a child played, tossing his wooden ball among the daisies and the lavender of the meadow, rolling a hoop, fashioned from the very green branch of a newly risen sapling, about. Chasing the birds in flight, their beaks full of the straw that might line a nest or the worms and the insects they carried to feed their young. Or, when he tired of the chase, menacing the hares and the newly hatched peepers with the small, tin sword he got on Beltaine.

Though he had been born to Valeda, Venutius and Alaina had watched over him as well. His three years had brought him a sturdy frame, long red locks, and eyes the blue of the Devon River. He rose every morning before the sun to do his chores. Gathering the eggs from the henhouse, and holding the pail for Alaina while she milked the goat he had christened Dania.

Alaina was in the fields with her newly-joined husband Morgaan, the son of a local farmer whose ancestors had plowed the earth around the dwelling where he had reached manhood for centuries. Though Alaina had been somewhat of an outcast when she had reached the lands that Venutius had brought them to north of Briton and out of the reach of the Romans, Morgaan had been taken by her spitfire ways, her determination to help Venutius pull from the land, once barren and filled with stones and clods of unforgiving clay, the wheat that put the bread upon their table and the flax that as spun linen clothed them. Though quiet, but firm, he had convinced his parents, over the objections of the local farmers and most of his kinsmen, to accept her as his wife.

The dwelling that stood behind Venutius' bench was ample, a room which had held a simple bed for Alaina and Valeda, and a smaller one for the child who was called Galyth. A great room, where Venutius slept, with a large, open fireplace that gave them warmth against the fairly mild winters, and an open pit, with a spit, to roast the fish and small game they supplemented their diet of milk and cheese, eggs and freshly baked bread with.

A small room had been added as a sleeping room for Alaina and Morgaan, built mostly by Morgaan, who had helped his father and his kinsmen add rooms and patch the thatched roofs that kept them from the many rains that fell upon the area. A small kitchen and pantry finished off the great room at the far end where Valeda prepared most of their daily meals.

Valeda was now nineteen, slender in build, with the palest of long, blond tresses and eyes as blue as a cloudless sky on a still, sunny day. She was known as a very young widow by the locals, the farmers and their wives, and the few traders who inhabited what might have passed for a village a few days travel away. Venutius did little to dispel this notion as he made his occasional neighborly rounds or traveled to barter for supplies. The truth of Galyth's birth was known only to Venutius and the two princesses.

As Venutius chiseled, Galyth dropped his play to run toward him, putting his chin on Venutius' knee. "Venutius," he asked, "when will my warrior be ready?"

Venutius chuckled. "As soon as we wrest his arms and legs from this block of wood," he answered, taking time to ruffle the boy's fiery locks, warmed from the morning's sun.

"What will he be called?" asked Galyth, pulling away to seat himself alongside the legs of the bench.

"Whatever you call him," answered Venutius, "for he will be yours to christen."

"Then, I will call him Venutius," he said, his face brightening with a certainty only a three-year-old could possess.

As they spoke, the door of the dwelling behind them was flung open. Valeda, clad in a pale, lilac tunic, the hue for which she plucked the hyacinths herself, walked toward them. Her tresses were pulled back by a single strand of linen. About her neck hung a small grey-black facsimile of a pony, held by a length of leather, carved from the shard of a very soft stone, uncovered by Venutius' plow the year of their very first harvest.

"Galyth," she called, laughing to see the boy jump up, "it is time for our noonday meal. You must run and get Alaina and Morgaan."

As he ran off, his form disappearing in the grasses before them, hoping to beg a ride atop Morgaan's shoulders on the journey back, Valeda turned to Venutius. "Alaina seems so happy now that she is joined with Morgaan," she said. "Will I ever be joined?"

Venutius put down his carving knife, returning her gaze, her eyes filled with a sparkle that seemed to reflect the noonday sun. "I'm sure that when the time is right," he answered, "the young lads about will be vying to make you their wife." He paused, searching the horizon, hearing the sounds of voices and laughter, mixed with the song of the birds nesting in the tree. "They return," he said, as he rose. "I will help you set out the noonday meal."

Alaina and Morgaan sat on three-legged stools on one side of the long, pine table set in front of the open hearth, Venutius and Galyth on the other, as Valeda brought cheese, bread and milk to set before them. Alaina spoke. "Venutius," she said, as she looked at her plate to fill it with a slab of the creamy goat cheese and a generous portion of the wheat bread she tore from the freshly baked loaf, "you must come to the fields to see how Morgaan and I have made ready the fields to sow the wheat. If Sequanna favors us this harvest, we shall have much to store against the winter when the goose and the partridge are scarce. Perhaps even enough to barter for a newborn hog."

Venutius smiled. "That will cost us much in stores of wheat," he said, as he too filled his plate with a hearty slab of cheese. "But, I will join you and walk behind the plow when you are ready to sow the first seeds of wheat and flax."

Then, Morgaan spoke. "Valeda," he said, as he looked at her helping Galyth to cut a slab of cheese, "when the wheat stands tall bending gently in the breeze my kinfolk will travel to thank the gods and attend the feast of Lhughasa. We would like you to go as well."

The invitation brought a flush to Valeda's otherwise pale countenance and an excitement she hadn't known since they had settled into the solitude of the land. But, duty and responsibility began to cloud her thoughts.

"Go, Valeda," said Venutius. "I will pull the milk from Dania and separate the curd from the whey. Then, when it is ready, I will stir the curd and coax it into cheese."

"Oh, please go," echoed Alaina. "We will take Galyth, and he will find lads as he to spin the ball and chase across fields to tag."

As Valeda happily consented, Alaina's and Valeda's giggly chatter filled the room. What costumes to take. What blossoms to gather to dress their tresses. An offer from Alaina to share the leather strand of many-hued stones Venutius had fashioned for her day of joining.

Then, Valeda turned to Galyth. "If we are to go, I must begin weaving your costume for Sanheim," she said. "What shall you be?"

"I shall be a warrior," he answered, "like Venutius. I must have the fiercest gods about my costume, then I will scare the evil spirits."

"We will pick the gods together," she answered, gently wiping the traces of Dania's milk with a linen cloth from about his lips. "Then, we will make up the tales we will tell beneath the moonlight."

Alaina pushed back her stool. "We must return to the fields," she said, as she rose. "The sunlight seems never as long as the work to plow."

She flung open the door, Morgaan right behind her. They laughed as they chased each other across the grasses of the meadow.

Galyth rose and burst through the open doorway. Perhaps he would catch a fish for the evening meal. A speckled trout or a plump, pink salmon.

He raced across the meadow, toward the valley below, where the rushing waters of a small, clear stream wound around a dale of the lush, green grasses of spring, filled with the newly-risen pale blue blossoms of the milkwort, and the bright, golden yellow of the buttercup. As he ran, his sturdy, chubby legs carrying him swiftly down the hillside, his red locks flowing in the breeze, his tinkling laughter echoed amongst the hills.

Author's Endnote

Boudicca's uprising was the last of many undertaken by the Celts against their Roman conquerors both on the European continent and in the British Isles. After building a structure called Hadrian's Wall, a feat of engineering with checkpoints every quarter mile named for the Roman emperor, to contain the conquered tribes against the fierce, unconquered tribes of the north, the Romans left the British Isles four hundred years later to answer problems at home. The Angles and the Saxons rode into the vacuum, unchallenged by the Celts, now placated by centuries of "Romanization".

Their spirit survives in the tales of the Welsh and the Irish, in the maypole dances of children throughout the world, and in the witches and goblins of All Hallows Eve, or Halloween. But, the Celts as a civilization never rose again.